Torn but Not Broken 2 "Peaches Revenge"

A Novel By

Lynaia Jordan

Lynaia Jordan

Lynaia Jordan

Acknowledgements

This book is dedicated to my little brother Donnell "Pop" Delbridge Jr. I remember when I was growing up, you were my shadow. I felt like you looked up to me. I know I did somethings not to a big sister's standard but one thing I know for sure is that I will and have always loved you so much! May you continue to Rest In Peace Little Brother! Gone but Never Forgotten! August 6, 1991 – January 28, 2017. My Favorite Aunt Doll-Doll the love I have for you is unconditional! You taught me so much, I never thought you were going to leave me. May you continue to Rest In Peace June 19, 1955 – June 30, 2017. My Little Cousin Ray Glasgow III you had your whole life ahead of you and one person's mistake rocked the whole family, watch over us RGIII October 9, 2000-May 5, 2018. My Big Brother Deandre Williams, our relationship was short lived, but I was so glad that I could call you my brother. Gone but Never Forgotten! March 25, 1980 – November 5, 2018. My father Maurice "Happy" Royster, thank you for the time we shared, may you rest in peace March 5, 1962 – December 19, 2018. With all the loss I have taken in two years, I will make my writing remember you guys forever! Always in my Heart!

Lynaia Jordan

Lynaia Jordan

Previously in Torn but Not Broken

Once I read the letter, I knew what Clyde wanted. Was I ready to give up Meth and start over with this man forever? It was a lot to take in and I really needed to talk to my momma before I make any drastic decisions that would affect my life forever. I called my mother and told her that me and the twins were coming over to visit her for a couple of days.

"Sun, you know you don't need no invitation to come bring my babies here. I miss all of you so and can't wait to see yall."

I knew after I had the twins my mother was concerned about my relationship with Meth. I insured her that I was going to be ok. She was not too thrilled about me moving to Georgia, but when I tell her that Meth was no longer a part of my future she would be thrilled.

"Mommie."
"Sun, baby, I missed you so much, and let me see them babies."

My mother grab Meshun, she always had a soft spot for the girls. When we walked in the house it really brought back memories. Like the first time me and Meth talked. I put down Jr. and went upstairs to my room. My mother left everything the same. I opened the door and looked around, and all I could see was the fifteen and sixteen-year-old girl

I used to be. I went over to my dresser and found my diary. As I read through, it brought back memories of me and Ruby. I began to cry. I missed her so much! My mother called me because the kids were hungry. I got up and took one last look at everything I was going to give away for a new life in Georgia.

After we feed the babies and put them down for a nap, I began to tell mother about the move, the new baby, and Clyde.

"Well, Sun, it is your life, baby, and I trust your judgment. I am happy that Meth is out of your life, but I hope that he will be there for the babies because they are the ones that need him most. You know when you were a little girl your father left, and I met your stepfather. He loved you and took on the role of being your father.   When   Joy came along it was nothing new to him because he was already a dad. I love you, Sun, and I know you will be ok, baby."

Me and my mother hugged, watched a movie, and got ready for dinner. We always wanted to go out together, so that night my stepdad had the kids and mom and I had a girl's night out.

"Mommie, can I talk to you about something?"

"Of course, Sun what is it?"

"I know that you don't promote violence, but before I leave Baltimore, I want to whip Peaches' ass. Not because I am mad about the baby, but because I am hurt that she tried to ruin and take my life."

"Sun, I am not going to tell you to go ahead and beat her ass, but I am not going to stop you, either."

We laughed. My mother was a strict person on not driving after you have been drinking, so we caught a cab home. I slept in my bed knowing that I would leave Baltimore and all that I knew forever.

Three days passed and we had been with my family. I wanted to give Meth some time to be with the kids before we left, so when I got home, I gave him a call.

"Hello."

"Hey, Sun, what's up?"

"I wanted to know if you wanted to see the kids before we left."

"Yeah, umm, I will be out tomorrow for the baby's two-week appointment, can I come afterwards?"

"We are leaving tomorrow, and I have a lot to do, so tonight will be good."
It burned me up inside to talk to him like that, but he never had to tell me about that baby.
"Sun, I am sorry. I will be there tomorrow to see my kids and that's the time I have."

I hung the phone up on him. That time I didn't cry. I called Clyde and asked if he could come over before I met him the next day on the field.

"Hey, baby, how are you feeling?"

"Since you asked, I am pissed. Meth pissed me off and I honestly want to beat the shit out of Peaches."

If I had a million dollars for the looked that was on Clyde's face after I went off, it was too funny.

"If you want to whip that ass, this the best time as any!"

I stared at him.

"I mean, why not? You all packed up and everything is ready to go, right?"

"Yeah."

"Then tomorrow before we leave, go over there whip her ass, and then we leave. I rented a truck for us to drive down in, and you can take my car and meet me at my place when you are done. I will have the kids and Ria with me."

I was shocked, but I loved it. I was going to whip that ass!

Clyde stayed with me that night and it was lovely. When I woke up, he was gone, and Ria was ready to get on the road.

"Ria, is everything we need for the twins in the truck?"

"Yeah, girl, we just waiting for you to come. It's almost twelve."

Lynaia Jordan

Oh shit, Clyde wanted me to meet him at twelve. I jumped in the shower and was ready to go. I made sure everything was locked up. I walked out the door and took one last look at my place and was tired and ready to move on.

"Sun, what do you have on, girl?"

"Oh, just some comfortable clothes, you know we have a long ride."

"Girl, you look like you are ready whip somebody's ass."

We pulled up at the field and it was a little league team practicing. I asked the coach if he knew Clyde, he said yes, pointed out in the middle of the field, and there he was. I waved and he began to run toward me, but so did the players. As they all came closer, they had letters on their shirts, not numbers, and it said,
SUN, WILL YOU MARRY ME?

I looked behind the kids and he was kneeling down in the dirt with a box in his hand. I turned and my mother, stepfather, Ria, and my babies stood there smiling. I turned to Clyde, and said, "Yes."

In my mind, I reacted fast but, in my heart, he was a great guy, we got along well, and he really cared about me. Clyde stood up, put the ring on my finger, and kissed me. The ring was BADD! I hugged my mom and dad and asked them did they know. My stepdad said Clyde called him and asked him for his permission to marry me. Right then and there, I said all my goodbyes and told my mother I was going to be ok. She said she knew. I was so happy. When we got in the truck, I was all smiles!

"Sun, could you do me a favor?"

"Of course, honey anything!"

"First thing is, love me forever. Second thing is, can you take my car to pick up this package for me?"

I knew exactly what he meant. I got out the truck and got in his car. I called Meth to see where he was, he didn't answer. I decided to go to Peaches' house and wait in front of her door. About an hour passed and they were coming down the street. I waited for them to pull up and then I got out the car. First Meth got out and asked me what I was doing there. I told him that I needed to talk to him and Peaches to get some things cleared up.

"Ok, Sun, but let me take the baby in the house." I asked him if it was ok for me to see the baby. He brought the baby over to me and I almost died inside. I keep my composure and tears inside.

When he came back outside, I knew I had to start the conversation off by telling them thank you.

"Well, Meth and Peaches, I want to thank you for making my life a living hell. Meth, I loved you so much with all of my heart and you tore it right out my chest because of this bitch Peaches. I wanted to let you know that your first-born son and daughter are going to be ok. I am getting married and I have a new home thanks to you. I hope y'all are happy and live a very dysfunctional ass life. Oh, and, Peaches, for the record, I will always be number one in his book, bitch!"

When I turned around to walk to the car, I heard her laugh, and say,
"Bitch, I'm glad you are leaving because it will be one less thing we have to worry about."

That was what I was waiting for. I turned back around and walked to her, and before she could open her mouth to ask me what's up, I banged her ass in the mouth and began to whip that ass. It took Meth about three minutes before he grabbed me and took me to the car. She was still lying on the ground crying, waiting for him to come to her rescue.

When he opened the car door, he said, "Sun, I am sorry. I never meant to hurt you and I love you with all my heart! Oh, you whipped that ass, baby!"

When he backed up, he had the biggest smile on his face. I put the car in drive and pulled off, laughing in the inside because I knew I won. I called Clyde let him know that I was on my way and we could hit the road. When I pulled up to Clyde's house, he was waiting in the driveway.

"Baby, are you ok?"
"Yeah, baby, I am good."
"Are you ready to hit the road?"
"Clyde, with everything that is in this Flaghouse

woman."

As we drove down 95, all I could do was began to let go of my past and look forward to the future. I knew it would be special because I intended to make it that way.

Lynaia Jordan

Prologue

Torn but Not Broken Part II

We lived in Georgia for two years and Meth hasn't called me one time. Maybe him and Peaches were living a happy life together. I try not to worry about the things that went on in Baltimore. I have a lot of painful memories and I am really trying to let that go. Now that I have moved on, I have a husband that loves me, kids that loves him and my best friend who will always be in heart and really been there with me through all the drama.

I decided to give my husband a birthday party. He is a well-known man in Georgia, so everyone who is somebody will be in the house. He party is going to be at the hottest spot in Atlanta. Everything was together and the final touches would be made later.

"Baby, are you ready?"
"Yes, Clyde, I am kissing the kid's good night and then I will be right down."

He is so excited. When I reached the bottom of the stairs, I remembered that I left my phone sitting on Mee-Mee's bed, so when I turned around, he instantly asked "What Now baby?"
I just laughed and went to get my phone, kissed them again and headed to the steps when I noticed I had a text message.

Lynaia Jordan

It read:
I will be there to claim what's rightfully mine. No matter how long it takes, we will be back together as a family.

My heart dropped and I dropped the phone down the steps.

Clyde asked, "What's wrong baby is everything ok?"
"Yes, baby I was just moving too fast that's all. Everything is fine."

After two years he wanted to talk this bull shit! I deleted the text message and prepared myself to celebrate my husband's birthday party with family and friends. In the back of my mind I couldn't really stop thinking about Meth. Why is he trying to ruin my life? Why he just can't leave us alone. I have to pull myself together I just have to. Clyde reached his hand out to grab me and give me a kiss I backed away a little because I felt guilty thinking about Meth. I know he is going to try and show up in my life again and once again my heart will be torn!

Chapter One

Sun

The ride to the club was quiet; Clyde was sitting next to me with a huge smile on his face showing all his beautiful white teeth. All I could think was that I was the luckiest woman in the world. I have a loving husband and two beautiful children. When we pulled up to The Mood Lounge, they had everything laid out for us. We had red carpet, lights, and escorts. I felt like a movie star, when the guy came to open the door of our yellow Porsche, I was bombarded by people trying to take pictures of me stepping out. I had on a red form fitting strapless Christian and Dior dress. This dress had boss written all over it. No one could tell me any different.

Clyde walked next to me and put his arm around mine and we walked the red carpet together. When we stepped in the room all eyes were on us. The D.J. gave him a shout out as soon as he walked in the door.

"Here comes the man of the hour our boy Clyde, Happy Birthday Clyde." said the D.J.

Whispering in my ear Clyde said "Sun I want to be the first man in this place to tell you that you look amazing. You are the most beautiful woman in the room."

Lynaia Jordan

He kissed my cheek and walked off to talk to some of his friends. I looked across the dance floor and I spotted Ray sitting in the VIP section. When I walked across the floor, I could feel all eyes on me. So, you know I had to put a little sexy twitch in my step. When I walked up on Ray it seemed like I scared her.

"Hey Ray"

"Hey Sun, girl I didn't even see you standing there."

"Yeah we just got here."

"Sun this place is very nice. I know Clyde is so happy. You even got his sister to come here from Baltimore that was nice of you."

"Yeah, well I try to keep them close when I can. He hardly gets to see his family with him jumping up and moving to Georgia with me. Ray is everything ok? It seems like you have something on ya mind?"

She turned and looked me dead in my eyes "Sun, I did something I shouldn't have, but I felt like it was the right thing to do at the time."

She had a scared look on her face, "Ray come on tell me, does it have anything to do with me and Clyde?"

"Yes Sun, Umm, Look I'm gonna just tell you cause you need to know. Yesterday Meth called the house when yall was out and he asked if he could speak to you. I told him you were out, and you would be back a little later. He asked me if you had a cell phone number. I gave it to him.

2

He said he wanted to talk to you about him coming down to see the kids. Sun I am so sorry if I caused any trouble. He tried to get the address, but I told him that was up to you if you let him have it."

"Ray that's cool, Meth didn't call but he did send a text
message tonight. I will call him tomorrow but tonight we party
for Clyde. Come on girl let's have a good time!"

We walked over to the bar.

"Ray what are you drinking?"
"Girl you already know"

I looked at the bartender and asked for a bottle of Ciroc and a pineapple and cranberry juice sent to the VIP section. The D.J. started to play Baltimore club music and me and Ray
was on our way to the dance floor. Ray had on this white Giorgio Armani pants suite with royal blue pumps and a royal blue bra showing just enough cleavage to get someone's attention. When we stepped out on the dance floor, we owned it.

All I seen was us back in the day at a party in the little rec center. I looked up and Clyde was watching my every move from the balcony. I began to move my hips a little harder because I knew he was watching. Me and Ray danced for the next two songs then we went to have a seat

3

and a drink. Clyde walked over to the VIP section and asked me if I wanted to dance.

"Baby, you know that I am not as young as I use to be, lol but yes, baby I would love to dance with you."

He turned to the D.J. and snapped his finger and he put on R. Kelly's "It seems like you're ready"

I had the biggest smile on my face because my husband was the sexiest man in the building, and he chose me to be his queen. He grabbed my hand and pulled me close to him. I could smell the cologne he had on. It was something new, but it smelled oh so good.

I whispered in his ear "baby what you have on?" And seductively he whispered back "Curve."

As we danced, he began to move his hands all up and down my body, I knew that feeling he was ready to go. Once the song went off, I asked him was he ready and he said yes. I walked over to Ray and told her I would see her in the morning.

"Sun yall is crazy but I'm happy that you are in crazy love the good kind!"

Ray smiled at me gave Clyde a hug wished him happy birthday and we exited the building. As we were waiting for the valet to bring the car, I looked across the street and I thought I seen somebody I knew. I could have sworn it was Meth. I had to take another look because I felt my stomach doing turns. I looked again and the person was gone. What the hell it must be the drink because I am seeing shit. I must have squeezed Clyde's hand hard because he asked "Baby are you ok? It looks like you just seen a ghost."

"Clyde baby I am fine I think I had a little too much to drink."

"Ok baby, just making sure my baby is good. Do you still want to go to the boat?"

"I'm ok Clyde, I just need to take a shower and lay with my husband."

He gave me a kiss as the car was pulling up. On the way there I fell asleep. Clyde woke me with a soft kiss to my lips. The captain was waiting with a dozen of roses and a bottle of champagne. Clyde had the room set up like it was my birthday.

"Sun, when you became my wife you made me the happiest man on earth. I love everything about you baby. You are strong, beautiful, a great mother, an excellent cook and not to mention you got the bomb!"

He had a big smile on his face when he said that.

"Sun all I want is for us to be together and raise the twins with morals. I know I am not their biological father,

5

but I love them just as much as Meth! With that being said I want to ask you could we try to have a baby."

"Clyde I would love to, in fact we could start tonight, but first let me go and take a shower and put on something more
comfortable like my birthday suite for your birthday!"

All he could do is smile I told him I was going to call and check on the kids and then I was getting in the shower. When I looked down at my phone, I had another text message from Meth.

*J Sun first thing I want to tell you the older you get the more beautiful you look. I am sorry that I haven't been here for the kids these past two years, but I would like to be here for now on. I know you and Clyde is happy, as much as it hurts me to
say this I'm glad you are happy. I'm still gonna get my family back and have you as my wife. I will call the house tomorrow once I see you are there... Oh you were killing them tonight in that red dress! It brought back so many memories! Have a good night Sun!*

I knew I saw him; I knew I wasn't crazy. I am going to have to tell Clyde but not tonight I am going to enjoy this night with my husband. I have to clear mind of Meth right now. I can't though, I thought he wasn't gonna try to come back in the picture I guess I was wrong.

Chapter Two
Meth

As I look at my son Melik, he was getting bigger every day. I took him to see Peaches every week. I didn't write her or send her any money. She deserves to pay for everything she did to me and Sun. It's coming up on the twins third birthday and I really miss my babies. The only time I get to see pictures is when Sun sends them up here to my cousin Ria. I show Melik pictures of his brother and sister and tell him that they love him very much. I have to figure out how I am going to get my family back. I know that Sun has a soft spot still in her heart for me, but I just don't know to make her see that I am the one for her and she is the one for me. I have to get her number from Ria, I am going to call Sun and ask her if I could still be a part of the twins' life. I got Melik together and then we headed to the salon to see Ria.

"Hey Ria, I need to talk to you for a second."
"Ard Meth let me set her hair and I will be ready to talk. Go sit in my office with Melik."

I haven't been in her office in years. I forgot that she keeps everything and put picture up everywhere. She had pictures of the twins. Sun. Ruby, Cory, my mother and father, Melik, Me and Sun was the one I couldn't take my eye off. Sun looked so beautiful and happy on this picture. I miss her so much. Ria snuck up behind me and whispered in my ear "You miss her, don't you?"

I turned to my cousin and said "Yes, Ria I miss her like crazy.
She means so much to me. I miss my babies. Ria I need to talk
to Sun. I need for you to give me her house number."

Ria stood there for a second before she said
"Look Meth, I don't want to get in the middle of your shit. Sun has moved on and has been raising those babies for two years without you. Cuz, you chose Peaches over Sun, even though I know you had a plan, but you still did it. I don't want you to go and bring drama to her life again she has been through enough
already Meth."

"Ria, I'm not trying to do that, I just want to know if I could be a part of my kids' life. I want them to meet their brother and I want them to get to know me. I promise I'm not going to do anything to mess up her marriage."

Ria gave me a look then she said ok, she gave me Sun's home number. I had to figure out what I was going to say to her and how I was going to react to what she had to say. I put the number in my pocket and then I continued with my day. Today was the day I took Melik to see Peaches.

Lynaia Jordan

"Hello, Peaches"
"Hi, Meth"

With a smile on her face she reached out for Melik.

"Hey man, Mommy misses you. Are you being a good boy for daddy?"
Melik said "Yes,"

He knew how to talk good for a two-year-old. Peaches kissed him and then looked at me.

"Well Meth, you know I come home in eighteen months, have you thought about us getting together to raise Melik?"

"Look Peaches, I told you I am not going to ever be back with you. I am not going to take Melik away from you either. He will live with me and you will be able to visit him. You need to work on your inner self. The shit you did to me and Sun was
unforgivable. I would have never thought you would stoop so
low. I forgave you Peaches but I also know you needed to pay, and your cousin needed to pay too. He lucky he is still breathing."

Lynaia Jordan

She seen the anger on my face, and she said "Look Meth, I am sorry for what I did. I did it because I was hurt. I loved you.

The time that I have been away from you and my son has made me realize I have to change my ways. I turned my life around Meth. I want to be better for my son. I want him to be proud of me. I miss Lil Earl too. Earl won't even let me see him or talk to him." Peaches began to cry.

"I am not a monster, it hurts me to see her really hurting, but she brought it on herself."
"Peaches, I see the changes you have made. I can tell just by how you talk to me. That's good but that doesn't change what
you did. I honestly wish you the best in your life, but I'm not going to be the one you are going to be with."

Peaches wiped her face and continued to play with our son and then our visit was over but before she got up to go in the back, she looks me in my eyes and told me she would love me forever and she forgave me too!

Melik and I stopped at Friendly's got some burgers, fries and ice cream and headed in the house. After we ate, I gave him a bath and put on his favorite cartoon, he was done for the night.

When I laid back on my bed, I thought about everything I wanted to say to Sun. I also thought about every reaction she could have had. I prepared myself for the worst. I got up took a shower and then in the morning I was going to call her.

The next morning, I decided to wait until I feed Melik to call Sun. Time flew by before I knew it, it was going on one o'clock in the afternoon and Melik was ready for his nap. So, I put him down and then I called her.

"Good Afternoon is it possible I can speak to Sun."
"Sun is not in; can I take a message?"
"Um, yes is it possible you can tell her that Mr. Methon Washington is trying to reach her."
"Meth is that you?"
"Yeah it's me, who is this."
"It's Ray, wow I am shocked, you got some balls."

When she said that I knew what kind of reaction to expect from Sun. Oh well! I laughed a little then I said "Well ray is it any way you could get in contact with her. I really need to talk to her about the babies. "When he said that I knew he really wanted to talk.

"I have her cell phone number, look Meth send her a text and tell her who it is and see if she calls you back. Please don't call her and have her off guard."
"Ok Ray, thanks I will text her. Hey Ray, how is my babies doing?"
"Meth, they are big and beautiful, especially Meshun, she is a mixture of you and Sun. She has your eyes and

Sun's hair. She is beautiful. Lil Meth he is a little man, a real good boy
undercover bad ass too."

"Ray I seen a picture of them in Ria's salon, but I can't wait to hold them I missed so much time. *My eyes began to water because I knew it was because of my actions I missed out on the twin's life.* Well that's enough chit chat, I will text Sun and see how she responds. Thanks, Ray, for everything."

" No problem. Talk to you later."

Once I hung up the phone my mind began to race. I called Ria and asked her if she could hold Melik for me for a little while. I explained to Ria that I didn't want to just take Melik to Georgia. She understood and told me whatever I needed her to do she was there. So that night I packed up a couple of my things and I left on the next thing smoking to Atlanta. When I arrived, it looked just as beautiful as when I left. I got a nice suite in the Marriott Hotel for a week and then I text Sun.

Lynaia Jordan

Chapter Three
Clyde

Waking up this morning looking in her beautiful face lets me
know that I had it all. I am going to stop at nothing to protect my family. Just the thought of that nigga being in Atlanta makes me sick, He hurt my baby and she didn't deserve it. Sun is a good woman and I know that I am the best man for her. I'm going to wait and see if he tries to contact Sun. I have to take Meth out the picture if he hurts my Sun again.

"Sun, wake up baby I have a surprise for you."

I kissed her softly on her lips then I whispered wake up in her ear. I know that she heard me but obviously she wanted me to do more. So, I moved the covers back to expose her beautiful caramel skin. I wanted to take my time this morning with her, so I began to kiss and suck her toes. I started from the pinky and nibbled on her big toe. Which was perfectly manicured?

When I licked the back of her calf, she made a small moaning sound, so I continued to the inner part of her thigh. See I did this because I knew she was ticklish there. When my tongue touched her thigh, she began to laugh.

Lynaia Jordan

"Stop Clyde, Stop!"

I paid her no mind because I love to hear her call my name. I didn't want to give her what she wanted so fast, so I laid next to her and looked her in her eyes.

"Sun, it's still my birthday baby can I ask you a question?"

She sat up a little and had this serious look on her face.
"Yes, Clyde you know you can ask me anything."

"Well baby, since we are in the mood, I wanted to know if you could lick my nipples."

When those words came out my mouth, we both laughed, I really couldn't resist. She always was so serious about everything I needed to make her laugh before I made love to her. She leaned over and said, "Your wish is my command!"

Sun began to lick around my nipples and moving like I was hitting it from the back. I couldn't let her do all the work, so I flipped her over and began to lick her nipples. The whole time talking to her and asking "Do you like this Sun? Is this what you want?" She just moaned yes to everything. For the next hour we made love none stop. When we were done, I laid my head on

Lynaia Jordan

Sun stomach and said to myself that I would protect her always.

Once we got out of bed, I wanted to do something fun with her. We jumped on the highway and went to Six Flags. We had the best time. We took pictures with the characters, played games and rode the rollercoaster. Sun was so scared, but she looked so cute screaming at the top of her lungs! By the time we made it back home it was around eight-thirty, the kids were feed and ready for bed.

We took a shower and Sun said that she needed to talk to me about something. I saw the worried look on Sun's face and automatically I had a bad feeling in the pit of my stomach.

Lynaia Jordan

Chapter Four
Sun

The whole ride home I was trying to think of a way to tell Clyde that Meth is in town. I know that I have to tell my husband about him texting me, but I don't know how he is going to react. I know that Clyde loves me, but I also know that he doesn't like to play games. I have to tell him, and I have to tell him tonight! When I walked out the shower, I saw my husband sitting on the bed looking so sexy. I knew this was the right time to talk to him.

"Clyde, I need to talk to you about something."
"Ok, baby what is it?"
"Well, yesterday Meth texted me and said that he wanted to get his family back. Then when we were leaving out the club, I thought that I was going to going crazy, but I thought I seen him across the street watching us. I wasn't crazy he is here. He sent me a text message last night to confirm. Clyde, I just want you to know that you are the love of my life now and I am yours and only yours."

If looks could kill, Meth would be dead, my husband is a laid
back guy, he doesn't like drama but don't get me wrong he doesn't play.

Lynaia Jordan

"Sun, sit on my lap baby? "

As I moved in close to Clyde, I could feel his heartbeat, through his white fitted tee.

"Sun, I love you with all that is within me and with all that is within me I will protect you from anything and everyone that tries to hurt you. I don't like Meth! Baby, I don't make it my business to talk about niggas, but he is weak! Anytime he let a woman like you hurt the way you did. Sun, I made a vow to you and I am going to stand by that vow and whatever you decide I will be by your side one hundred percent baby."

Clyde kissed me and asked me if he could just hold me tonight. I kissed my husband back and that's what he did, held me all night.

I heard my phone ringing around nine. Clyde rolled over and told me it was an unknown number, so I answered it on speaker because I knew it was Meth.

"Hello"
"Good Morning Beautiful, can you talk?"
"Yes, Meth I can talk what's up?"
"Sun, I just want to know if I could come and see my kids."

I looked at Clyde to see what he thinks, and Clyde shook his head yeah.

"Yeah, Meth you can come and see them."

"Well can I come over now?"

"No Meth come around twelve. I have to get the kids together."

"Ard, sweetie, I can respect that I will be there at twelve."

The phone hung up and I turned and looked at Clyde to see what his reaction was. He was looking at me to see what my reaction was too.

"Clyde, are you ok?"

"Yeah baby, I'm good, make sure the kids are good and I will sit in the background. I will only step up if you need me."

"Thank you, baby, but I think I will be able to handle it!"

It was eleven fifty and I was so nervous. I haven't seen Meth in years, I know I wondered what I was going to do when I see him, but the time is now. I put a little yellow and white polo dress and sandals on Mee-Mee and lil Meth had on a polo T-shirt the same color as Mee-Mee dress with polo decks. I was fixing Mee-Mee hair when the door bell rung. As I walked to the door, I could see that Meth had flowers in his hand. When I opened the door, I was in love all over again.

"Hello Sun, you look good. Can I come in?"

I was stuck, Meth looks didn't change one bit. He was still that fine ass brown skin nigga; I was in love with.

"Hey Meth"

I reached in to give him a hug, but he gave me the flowers
instead.

"So, Sun where the babies?"
"Babies, Meth they are little people."

We both laughed. I walked him into the living room where the twins were. When Meth laid eyes on them his face expression was like he was getting ready to cry.

"Mee-Mee and Lil Meth come here I want you to meet somebody."

They both ran to me and gave me a hug.

"Look, who is this?"

Lil Meth said "That's my farva"

Methon picked him up while laughing and said "That's right man it's my daddy"

I don't think Methon was ready for the next thing that came out of lil Meth mouth.

Lynaia Jordan

"Hey, you not my dad, you my farva, Clyde is my dad."

"Lil Meth! I am so sorry Methon, Are you ok?"

"Yeah it's cool I haven't been here for them so how could I be his dad. By the way where is Clyde? He not here?"

I didn't see Clyde standing in the loft that overlooked the living room.

"I'm here Meth, how are you?"

"I'm good man; I want to thank you for taking care of my fa...
children while I was gone."

"While you were gone, you sound like you were doing a bit or something, you were right in Baltimore."

I saw the frustration in Clyde's face, so I was ready to cut in when Meshun ran and asked Clyde to pick her up. "Daddy pick up please."

Before Clyde picked up Mee-Mee he looked Meth in the eyes and then said,

"Sure, baby girl" then kissed her on her forehead.

Clyde looked over at me and I gave him a look and knew just what I was saying.

Lynaia Jordan

"Mee-Mee daddy has to make a run, but I will be back, I want you to stay here with mommy and your father ok."

"Ok daddy."

She gave Clyde a kiss on the cheek and then ran back over to me.

"Excuse me Meth for a second."

I walked Clyde to the car. Clyde turned to me before getting in the car and said

"Sun, that nigga was asking for me to say something. I know what I said earlier but I couldn't just sit there and not say something. Sun if he says anything out the way to you baby, I want to know." When he said that, he looked me in the eyes. I knew Clyde was serious so that's why I just gave him a passionate kiss and told him "Baby, I got everything under control."

When I walked in the house, I could hear Meth asking the kids questions and then the kids laughing.

"Meth would you like something to drink?"
"Yeah, what you got?"
"Alcoholic or Non-Alcoholic?"

21

Lynaia Jordan

We both smiled cause it took us back to when were in my living room. Before kids, Peaches and drama!

"Umm, Sun you can get me a glass of apple juice if you have it."

"Ok, we have apple juice, Mee-Mee and Jr. do you guys want something to drink?"

"Yes, mommy we want apple juice too."

When I walked in the kitchen, I heard Meth say to the kids, "Your mother is beautiful isn't she?"

Lil Meth answered fast "yes she is, she is the prettiest princess!"

Meth laughed and said "You got that right Jr."

I came back in the living room and noticed that my little princess was sad. I gave them their juice and then went over to Meshun and asked her what was wrong.

"Mommy I don't know him, I am scared. Mommy is daddy going away now?"

I picked my baby up and walked her into the kitchen. Looking at Mee-Mee was like looking in a mirror, she looks just like me, so I know that if she is my twin, she loves hard. I heart was hurting so bad to see her feel this way, but I had to explain it to my baby the best way I could.

Lynaia Jordan

"See Meshun, Meth is your father he just went away when you and Jr. was babies. I know you don't remember him, but he was there when you were born. Your Daddy Clyde has been with you since Meth went away. It's ok Meshun to get to know Meth ok. He is not going to hurt you."

Meshun gave me a hug and told me ok and ran back in the living room and began to play with Meth and Jr.

They played and laughed together all day he even told them about their little brother Melik and how he really wanted to meet them. I don't know when he started to talk about Melik I began to feel different about Meth and my heart began to feel that same pain it felt years ago. I looked at my watch and saw that it was going on five and the kids haven't eaten dinner.

"Hey, you guys, mommy want you to go upstairs and tell Ray-Ray to get yall ready for dinner ok."
"Ok mommy." They said.

So, they ran up the stair to find Ray-Ray. I turned to Meth and asked him to walk out back with me. He stood to his feet and agreed. As we started to walk the trail out back of my house, I began to talk to him.

"Meth, how have you been?"
"Sun, I have been ok, just incomplete that's all."

23

"How have things been with you and Peaches?"
"Sun, no one has told you what happened."

I stopped walking and looked at Meth, "Tell me what?"

"Sun, you mean to tell me that no one told you about Peaches"

I felt myself laughing in the inside, but then I gave him a serious look and said "Meth, what happened to Peaches?"

"Sun it's a long story but all you need to know is ya boy Keith is five O and Peaches is locked up."

Oh my god Keith the police and Peaches in jail. Well that part I was happy about, but Keith I was shocked.

"Meth you have to tell me everything."

"Ok sweetie, I will tell you everything but first I want to know, how are you? Is Clyde treating you like a queen? Have you forgiven me? Do you miss me Sun?"

I stopped walking and turned to face Meth and all I could feel is love in my heart for him. I love him so much and I know this feeling will never go away but I can't react on this feeling now. I just can't.

Lynaia Jordan

"Meth I am not ready to go there with you right now. I just can't. You know that Clyde is a good man, he stepped up and took care of your damn family when you abandoned us for Peaches, a bitch that didn't care about you worth a fuck!"

I began to cry because I was truly hurting inside.

"Meth I am so tired of your bullshit; you think that you can come into my life and try to pick up where you broke all the pieces! Well Meth you can't, I wanted to walk with you and take this time to let you know that me and the kids are doing well, we are happy, and we don't want ya drama ass life apart of ours. So If you think in any way that the things that are going on in your life is going to affect our children I want you to turn and walk away right now Meth and don't look back cause if you hurt us in any way again it will be your last time."

He was standing there with a smirk on his face and before I knew it, he was kissing me.

Chapter Five
Clyde

Driving down Cobb Parkway on my way to the gym to let off a little stress, I got a text message from Ray telling me that Sun and Meth took a walk out back. That really made me angry, but I trust my wife and I know that she loves me so no matter what she will respect me. When I walked into the gym, I went straight to my personal trainer Percy to see if he had some time for me.

"Hey Percy, you got some time for a brother I really need a workout."

"No problem C. You know you my best client. We could hit the weights first then we could do a 20-minute workout."

"Good Percy this is just what I need."

Now when we first moved to Georgia, I didn't know anyone. The first person I met was Percy and he has been a good friend to me down here. It's a small world because Percy went to grade school with Meth and his homeboy Mark. They weren't close friends, but he knew them. I feel real comfortable talking to Percy about Meth I know that I can trust him. Percy was a 26 years old husband and father of four and he could relate to a lot that I am going through with Meth and Sun.

"Look Percy, I know I said I need a work out but damn you trying to get me ready for the Olympics."

We both laughed because he knew I was telling the truth. While I was doing sit-ups, I started to tell him about Meth coming back.

"Yeah, he came to the house this afternoon and it made me so mad to see him look at my wife like he missed her and loved her so much. Percy I'm telling you if he tries anything with Sun, I am going to kill him."

"Hold, C Man don't even think like that Sun is your wife and I believe she won't even let him take it there with her. She doesn't even seem like that kind of woman."

"Percy, I know their history and for whatever reason it is Meth had a hold on Sun! He had her heart man I don't even know if she has ever really let go of the love, she had for him."

"Wow, well Clyde let me ask you something. Do you believe that your wife really loves you?"

"Yeah, I believe Sun loves me."

"Ok, did you let Meth know what the business was?"

"Naw, we had a couple of words and Sun butt in, but I think I have to let him know because I'm telling you if he tries anything, he's a dead man."

The look that I gave Percy made him not say another word, we just finished the workout. He told me to call him if I needed him. On my way back home, I stopped at the bar and picked me up a drink. I think tonight I might need one. I pray to God that he is not still at my house. I didn't receive a call from Sun, so I hope he is gone. When I walked through the door, I could smell my favorite food cooking and I knew he was gone.

"Baby, Baby where are you?" I yelled through the house.
"Clyde I'm in the kitchen."

I walked towards the kitchen and I saw my baby standing there in front of the stove with her my favorite nightie on and a pair of those purple leopard print stilettoes on! I had an instant hard on. She was the best and I knew I couldn't let her go for no one!

"Come here sexy let me see what you are cooking."

She laughed and turned to me with a little flour on her cheek.

"Baby, I think you need to go take a shower and get in bed. I will be right up with dinner."
"Sun, where is the kids"
"They are in bed; they will be out for the rest of the night and
Ray is gone over her boyfriend house, so we are all alone."

I got up out the chair and gave my wife a kiss and ran up the stairs. It's getting ready to be on! Oh, I hope she don't think that we are not going to talk but I am not yet done with talking about Mr. Meth. I want to know. I will wait because I have a gut feeling that I am not going to like what I hear but I am ready for it! I just pray that this nigga knows who he is dealing with. In the shower all I could think about was making love to my wife my dick was rock hard the whole time. After I got out the shower I dried off and got in the bed naked. I wanted Sun to see that I was ready for whatever she wanted to give. I sat up in our king size, sheep wool stuffed, and Persian marble bed. I could hear her heels coming down the hallway. My man stood at attention just knowing that baby was on her way to take care of daddy.

"Clyde is you ready for something good to eat baby?"
"Yes, I am!"

She walked through the door with a plate of chicken, green beans and rice and gravy my favorite, um my baby sure does know how to make her man happy. She feed me and then she
asked me "Are you ready for your desert?"

All I could say was yes baby, yes!"

Last night was amazing, I couldn't ask for another woman in a million years. I know that it was something on her mind because when we finally went to bed, she just laid there looking at the ceiling. I wanted to ask her what was wrong, but I didn't I just laid there wondering what she was thinking about.

When Sun got out the shower she came and sat on the edge of the bed and turned to me.

"Clyde baby I need to talk to you."

I sat up, "Yeah baby, what is it?"

She took a deep breath and then said "I know that you were giving my space yesterday when Methon came here to see the kids. I know how much it may have hurt you to see him here. I can't change that Meth is the father of the twins. Clyde, I don't want to deny him from seeing them. Baby yesterday seeing Meth again really brought back some painful memories for me."

Sun began to cry.

"Clyde, after he played with the kids for a while, I asked him to take a walk with me. We walked through the trail and we talked and listening to him and realizing how he hurt me, I knew that my love for Meth will never be the way it was when I was in Baltimore. Clyde before I could get everything off my chest to him, he kissed me."

"What the hell, Sun what do you mean he kissed you?"

"Calm down, Baby he kissed me on my lips, but I smacked him and I let him know that I am a happily married woman with a wonderful husband who loves me and our children to death and I am not jeopardizing that for no one not even him!"

Looking in Sun eye's I knew my baby was telling the truth and I knew everything was going to be ok.

"Listen Sun, I am glad you told me this, but I am mad as hell he did that to you."

"Clyde he won't be back anytime soon! Baby I let him know he has no family here. We are your family and if he can't accept that then he doesn't need to come around."

I kissed Sun on her forehead as she cried on my shoulder because I knew it hurt her to treat Meth that way, but she knew he was no good for her and the kids.

"Oh, Clyde I didn't tell you that Peaches is in jail and Meth has custody of their son who he asked me if we could raise him with the twins!"

I was shocked so I looked at Sun and asked her "So what did you say when he asked you that?"

"What the hell do you think I said? I said hell no. He and Peaches is going to raise their son not me and I be damned if he thinks he is going to bring him around me cause he not! I know honey that it is not the little boys' fault how his mother is, but I haven't gotten all the way over that yet! Sorry!"

Lynaia Jordan

"Baby I understand I don't want him here either. We need to focus on the twins and how we can give them the best life possible."

"I know baby and that is what I intend to so."
We kissed and then woke the kiss up so we could go get breakfast.

Lynaia Jordan

Chapter Six
Meth

Ten Years Later......

"Melik come on down here boy, I need you to take out the trash so we can make it to the carwash on time."

"Ard Dad, I'll be right down." Melik said

When I saw my son running down the stairs, I was so proud of the young man he was becoming. He was a tall brown skin pretty boy, he looked just like Peaches, but the only thing was he had my eyes.

"Dad, can we stop pass Shoe City so I could get the new
AirMax?"

"Melik you just got some AirMax last week. What you think
money grows on trees?"

"Dad, Lil Cory said these were the hardest out. Please?"

"Ok Melik, take out the trash and then we can stop. Hurry up boy we still have to pick up your mother. "

Melik took out the trash and then we headed down Harford Road towards the city. I knew Melik was ready to ask if I was going to pick up lil Cory so they could do a little work at the carwash. So, I just stopped and picked him up. When I got out the car, I saw a familiar face from the past.

"Hey, um what's your name? Sorry I can remember faces but names I'm not that good with."
"Meth it's me, Hedah, Sun's friend. How have you been?"

"Oh right, I've been good. I can complain. I just stopped by to pick up Lil Cory."
"Right his grandmother still lives here. Well I was just visiting a couple of people and passing out flyers for our fifteen-year class reunion. Hey by any chance would you be able to get in contact with Sun?"

When she asked me that it took me back to the last day, I saw her in the back yard. Sun wow, I haven't thought about her in years. Even though I send her child support for the twins we still don't communicate.

"Yeah, Hedah let me give you her number and Ray's too! You know they both live in Georgia now. As a matter of fact, Ray-Ray is getting ready to get married she told me."
"Cool, thanks so much Meth, keep up the good work and you still look good!"

I just smiled gave her hug and kept it moving. After I picked up Lil Cory, we picked up Peaches and then went to the Carwash, but the whole time I couldn't stop thinking about Sun. I'm glad that I and Peaches forgave each other and the time she did in jail really changed her for the better. She was a great mom and she also went back to school for nursing. Sometimes I can see the old Peaches trying to come out when I say something about the twins but then she catches herself and know that the only way we will remain friends if she keeps being the new Peaches. I went into my office and shut the door so that I could look at Sun's class reunion flyer. I am going to be there. I just haven't got over my queen. I fucked up bad and this will be the perfect chance for me to get her back.

"Melik, can you get mommy something cold to drink please?"

Peaches said Melik turned back and gave Peaches a look and then went into the back of the carwash. I saw Peaches look at me and then walked towards my office.

"Meth, what's wrong with Melik? For the past two weeks he has been really disrespectful to me."
"Peaches I have no idea, but I will have a talk with him. In the meantime, just give him a little space."
"Ok Meth, but I am going to give you until Sunday which is two days and then I am going to check his little ass. He must smell his piss and I am not the one."

I just laughed and then I told her ok. I walked to the back of the carwash where Melik and Lil Cory were cleaning out this Lexus LS430 for my homeboy.

Lynaia Jordan

"A Melik come here and let me talk to you for a minute."

I walked towards the back door and stepped outside. Melik followed me.

I turned to him and said, "Hey man, I noticed lately that you have been being really disrespectful to your mother. What's up with that?"

He had look on his face like he was getting ready to say something them he sat on the chairs out in the back. When I looked into my son's eyes, I had seen pain, so I told him to let it out.

"Dad, I was talking to Lil Cory and he told me that his granny told him stories about you, my mom and Ms. Sun. Some things I don't believe but some I do. Like why my mom was in jail and why you and her not together and why I never get to see Mee-Mee and Lil Meth. Dad do my mom have another son named Earl that is older than all of us?"

I wish this didn't come up now, but I have no other choice but to be honest with my son.

"Well Melik I was hoping we wouldn't have this conversation until you were like sixteen but since Cory big head tail wanted to share things with you then I am going to tell you everything now. Your mother does have another son that is fourteen years old his father name is Earl he was a guy your mother was dating. Then yes, your mother was involved in things that she is not proud of. But in no way did she ever stop loving you. You will see Mee-Mee and Lil Meth soon. To answer your question about me and your mother not being together, honestly son I am in love with Ms. Sun. I love your mother, but I am not in love with her. She knows this and we are good friends. It's a lot of other stuff you should know about but now is not the time. So, you go back in the carwash and go give ya mother a hug and let her know you love her."

He smiled and told me ok. Wow I can't believe that I just told my twelve-year-old son that I was in love with Sun. I am really gone but I will soon be back with my queen. After we took care of business at the car wash, we went out to eat then dropped Peaches off home and continued to our house. Lil Cory and Melik were in the back seat talking about what they were going to wear to the school dance. It made me remember when me and Cory use to make plans about what we are going to wear out to the club. I just smiled at the boys! It's seems like more lately I find myself thinking about my best friend. I hope that he is proud of me and how I look out for Lil Cory and his mother. When I pulled up at the house, I noticed that the lights were on in the living room. I never leave the lights on so I just kept on driving because I honestly don't know who that could be, and I definitely don't want to have my son in harm's way. When I pulled up at Lil Cory's house, I told them to keep

Lynaia Jordan

their cellphones on and I will be back later to get them. I jumped back in the car and went back to my house.

Now the lights are out! What the fuck. I went under my seat and got my nine. I got out the car and started to walk to the when I felt someone on my back. I turned around to find a big, tall, dark   skin nigga standing in my face looking just like Peaches. I pointed the nine in his face and said, "Nigga you better start talking or I'm gonna blow ya fucking head off."

"Um, um" The boy stuttered.
"Um, I am Earl, I broke in ya house because I didn't have nowhere else to go. This was the address my father gave me before he was killed. I was hiding in the closet when some men came in our house and killed him."

The young boy began to cry.

"They didn't try to find me. When they pulled off, I went over to my father he told me the name Peaches and this address. I really don't understand Mr. but I need your help."

I put the gun down and told Earl to come on I the house before the neighbors call the cops on me. I felt so bad for Earl because he was a cool dude. This is crazy, I have to call Peaches and let her know what's going on.

Lynaia Jordan

Peaches needed for me to come and pick her up. I told earl to wait at the house he will be safe there. I will be back in 15 minutes. When I picked, he up she was crying?

"Meth, I am so scared, I haven't seen him in so many years. Earl kept him from me. I tried to contact them he changed the number and moved. I didn't know they were living back in Baltimore. Meth, does he look like me?"
"Yeah Peaches he looks just like you."

We pulled up to the house, she couldn't stop crying.

"Peaches, I have to tell you one more thing. Um Big Earl never told him who you were, so he doesn't know you are mother."

Peaches just broke down in the driveway.

"Meth, what am I going to do, I fucked up my life, how can I ever come back from this GOD help me please!"

I walked over and lifted Peaches up from the driveway and told her "Peaches, you are better than you where ten years ago. You are strong and you are a woman now. Go in and tell ya son the truth, he needs to know you are all he has now so it's time to step up. I am here for you. Me and Melik you know that."

When she opened the door, she began to cry again and the look on Earls face was puzzled.

Lynaia Jordan

"Hey Earl, my name is Peaches"
"Hello Ms. Peaches. I guess Mr. Meth told you what happened. My father gave me ya name and this address and told me to leave and never look back."

Peaches began to cry harder and I told her to sit down.

"Well Earl, I think you need to sit down because Peaches needs to tell you a few things."

He sat on the couch next to Peaches and looked her straight in the eyes.

"Earl I am your mother. When you were a baby your father said he was going to go visit family and he never brought you back. I wasn't living the best kind of life to raise you in the first place. You have a brother and his name is Melik. I am so sorry Earl. Once I started to get my life together, I tried to find you, but Big Earl moved and changed the number. I am so sorry baby. I don't know what Earl told you but I Love You baby and I am here for you."

He just sat there looking in Peaches eyes then he turned to me then turned to Peaches and gave her a hug.

"Ms. ... Mom I knew he was lying, he treated me bad once I turned seven, he met this lady and that's when all his time turned to her. I used to be home alone all the time. I never complained because he made sure I had he just didn't

40

Lynaia Jordan

care about me. He never took me to the doctors or anything. I used to do everything myself. No one ever asked any questions.

Like four months ago Brooke left him and took everything. She left him with nothing that's when he moved back up here. I wasn't in school cause never took me to register me. I just stayed in the house and read books the whole time. Last week he got a phone call from this guy and I heard him yelling and saying F her. He slammed the phone down and told me to go in my room and stay there until he tells me to come out.

It was two days before he let me come out. My father started to use drugs once Brooke left. I know because I saw things lying around. Then yesterday I walked to the bathroom when he was lying out on the floor and beside him was a glass pipe and bags of white powder and rocks. I knew what it was the next morning I heard him fussing with two men I never came out the room, so they didn't know I was there. I heard three-gun shots and the door slam, and the car pull off. I walked to the stairs to see my father laying on the floor bleeding, I ran down stairs and he just said Son get out of here, go to Peaches 4210 Springwood Ave. find it she will take care of you.

I don't have anything anymore, but you will be ok. Never look back I love you son. I saw his eyes roll in the back of his head I knew he was gone. I ran up the stairs got my clothes and left never looking back. I don't know who or why they killed him, but I am glad he told me about you because I would have been lost."

Lynaia Jordan

Peaches grabbed her son and kissed him and told him he would be ok. She was here now. She held him and rocked him.

"Peaches and Earl, yall can stay here tonight. I will go and pick up Melik in the morning and we all can go out to get some breakfast ok."

The next morning, they were up early and ready. When Melik got in the car he looks at Earl and said to me "Dad this is who I was talking about yesterday isn't it? "

I laughed and said, "Yes son now sit back and chill we are going out to eat and talk."

Peaches shot me a look like what was we talking about, but I just smiled at her.

Chapter Seven
Sun

Back in Georgia.........

"Mee-Mee we are going to be late for the program."

When my baby ran down the steps all I could see was me when I was her age. Oh, but I see so much of Meth in her.

"Ma is Meth coming to the recital because I really don't want him to miss it."
"Yes, he and Clyde will be there."
"Ard, they better because the directors from the dance school will be there watching. I will need all the support I can get."
"Mee-Mee you will have your support, I just want you to go out there and do your best baby. You got this!"

She gave me a hug and we grabbed her bags and got in the car. While I was driving my cellphone rung and it was a Baltimore area code.

"Hello"

"Hello, can I speak to Sun."

Lynaia Jordan

"Yes, this is Sun."

"Hey Sun, it's me Hedah."
Oh my God, Hedah, I haven't spoken her name in
like eleven years.

"Hey, Hedah how are you is everything ok?"

"Girl yes I am doing fine, and everything is
wonderful. I got your number from Ray-Ray I hope you
don't mind."

"Don't be silly, I don't mind. So, what's up how's
everything?"

"Sun, everything is wonderful, but I was calling to
see if you could come to our fifteen-year class reunion?"

"Hedah, when is it?"

"It's next month, the kids will be out of school then
so I hope you will be able to come. I haven't seen the twins
since they were babies. I really miss you Sun."

"I miss you too Hedah, let me talk to the family and
I will call you back to let you know for sure. How much are
the tickets?"

"They are 20, but you don't worry about it if you are
coming just bring yourself."

Lynaia Jordan

"Alright, then, I'm glad you called me I will call you tomorrow to let you know."

"Ok Sun talk to you tomorrow."

"Ok"

When I hung up the phone, I was happy that she called but I really don't know if I want to go back to Baltimore, I am really not ready to face my past.
"Ma, who was that?"

"Remember I told you about the friends I had in Baltimore, she is one of them. She was one of my good friends."

"Ma you sure do look happy. Do you miss your friends and family back in Baltimore?"

"Sometimes I do but I love the family I have here."

"Well I think that we should go to visit, I have thinking about my father and I would like to see and meet my little brother. I know I don't talk about Methon much but I would like to know him a little better I am older now so I can understand things a little better."

Listening to Meshun talk I know that I am doing a great job with them.

45

Lynaia Jordan

"Ok Mee-Mee I am going to talk to Clyde tonight and I don't see why we not going to be able to go."

When we pulled up the parking lot was packed, and I was looking for Clyde's car, but I didn't see it maybe they were running late.

"Mee-Mee go head in start to get ready I will get some seats for us."

"Ok ma."

I gave her a kiss and wished her good luck. I grabbed my purse out of the car and started to walk towards the school when I felt a shadow come up behind me. I turned around quickly to see who it was, and it was Clyde and lil Meth.

"Dang Ma, I was trying to scare you!" said lil Meth

"Boy don't play with me like that. I was about to knock ya head off."

I leaned toward Clyde to get a kiss from him.

"So, fellas where are yall coming from?"

"Oh baby, we just came back from a double date with this fashion model and her fourteen-year-old daughter."

"Hahaha, very funny Mr. you could play with me if you like." I gave Clyde the evil eye.

"Sike baby we were at the gym then we decided to go grab a bite to eat before her recital."

When we walked into the auditorium and it was jammed packed. Lil Meth went and sat next to some of his homeboys and I and Clyde found two seats on the second row. I was so proud of my baby. I pulled out the camcorder and waited for the light to go out to begin recording.

Clyde leaned over and gave me a kiss and said, "Baby I love you so much, you are a wonderful wife and an excellent mother to our kids."

"Thank you so much Clyde for being a great husband and father to our kids. I love you very much as well."

Mee-Mee came out and did her thing I saw the scouts watching her and she was the best one out there I know she will be getting into the best school. After her recital we took her and her friend out to eat. Once we dropped off her friend, we headed home. Mee-Mee rode with me and lil Meth rode with Clyde.

"Mee-Mee do you need anything else before I go to bed?"

Lynaia Jordan

"No mommy I am good."

She walked up to me and gave me a big hug.

"Ma, I love you so much you are the best, I only wish my father was here to share my life with you. I really would like to start to get to ma."

She looked at me with sadness in her eyes, I know she misses Methon.
"Mee you can call Methon anytime you like. He will answer; I just thought that you and lil Meth didn't want to talk to him. Let's just go to bed tonight and in the morning, we will give him a call ok."

"Ok, goodnight ma."

"Goodnight baby, I love you too!"

I went in my room and lay across the bed waiting for Clyde and lil Meth to come in the house. They must have made a detour so something. As I was laying there my mind started to wonder and think about Meth. I snapped out my thought when I heard the front door open. When Clyde came in the room I sat up on the bed because I knew I wanted to talk to him about going to Baltimore for like a week to visit family and go to the class reunion.

"Hey Clyde, I need to talk to you about something."

Lynaia Jordan

He sat down on the bed next to me and then held my hand. Looking me straight in the eyes he said, "Well Sun what's on ya mind?"

"Well Clyde I wanted to know if we could go to Baltimore for a week to visit family and so I could go to my class reunion."

"Of course, baby, when is it. We could make the arrangements in the morning. I wanted to go see my mother anyway."

I gave him a smile because he really is an undercover mama's boy.

"Ok, then the next thing I want to ask you is if you could make love to ya wife tonight?"

"Come on now baby you know you don't have to ask a silly question like that."

I got up to go jump in the shower and asked him to look in the drawer and take out whatever he wanted me to wear tonight and put it on the bed. Once I was in the shower, I felt him jump in with me. He stood behind me and his dick rubbed up against my ass. I took my hair down and he began to kiss my back and my neck. I stretched my arms up on the wall and spread my legs apart. He licked and kissed my back and my ass finally turning me around to face him. Pushing me back so that the water could be my body

Lynaia Jordan

Clyde sucks my nipples; he knew this was my spot. He worked his way down. This felt like the first time we have been together. Once I poured out my emotions, I told him to lay back and gave him the best backwards ride of his life. I saw my husband toes curl, so I knew I was satisfying him.

"Clyde, I thought I asked you to get me something out you wanted me to put on."

"Baby, tonight all I want to see is skin, so I didn't put anything out."

I turned and looked at him and said, "Round two!"

He started to laugh, then grabbed me and slammed me on the bed. We made love all night long it was beautiful. The next morning, I was woken to breakfast in bed. It was delicious.

"Clyde did you make this, or did you order it from somewhere?"

"Sun now you know ya baby can cook. I just haven't been
because I have the best wife in the world."

"Well, this is the best breakfast I ate all year!"

I leaned over to give him a kiss. Once I finish eating, I got up put my clothes on and wanted to start my day by making arrangements for us to go to Baltimore. I book a flight, hotel and car rental arrangements for me, Clyde and the kids. Everything was set we will be in Baltimore in one month, now I have to go tell lil Meth and Mee-Mee was going on.

Yelling up the stairs "Meth and Mee-Mee come down here I need to talk to yall."

Mee-Mee ran down the stairs and when I didn't see lil Meth I yelled again them Mee-Mee said, "ma he left out early this morning."

"Oh really, well I will tell him later, but Mee we are going to Baltimore in a month."
"Ok, that's good ma but now can we call Methon so I could talk to him?"

"Ya we can but don't tell him we are coming up there in a month we can surprise him."

"Ok, come on let's call now."

I dialed the last number I had on him hoping that it didn't change.

"Hello"

"Hello, can I speak to Methon please."

Lynaia Jordan

"May I ask whose calling?"

"This is Sun."

It got quite on the phone for a second then he said something.

"Hey Sun, this is me, is everything ok?"

"Yes, Meth everything is fine, I was calling because Mee-Mee wanted to talk to you."

I gave Mee-Mee the phone and walked in the living room to give her some privacy. I walked over to the window to see lil   Meth get out the car and give Clyde a package, and then Clyde pulled off. My mind started to wonder, and I felt myself having a panic attack. I know he don't have my son mixed up in some bullshit. I ran up the steps to get my cellphone I needed to get some answers from Clyde.

"Hello, Clyde I need you to come home because I need to talk to you."
"Baby I will be back in like an hour."

"No Clyde I need you to come home now."

It got quite on the phone then he said, "Baby I'm on my way is everything ok?"

Lynaia Jordan

"No, Clyde it's not but I hope it will be. I will talk to you when you get here."

I hung the phone up and sat on the edge of my bed thinking. Before I knew it, tears were running down my face. I was feeling the same pain in my heart I felt when Meth was still fucking with Peaches. I know it is different things, but the thought still makes me feel the same way. Five minutes later I heard his car pull up in the driveway. I wiped the tears from my face and sat in the chair next to the window. When he opened the bedroom door, he saw me sitting next to the window. He walked over to me and knelled down.

"Baby what is it? Are you ok Sun?"

I looked Clyde in the eyes, and I said "I was looking out the window earlier and I saw Junior give you a package. Clyde was that about and why is junior leaving out early on the weekends and always underneath you. Clyde please tell me my gut feeling is wrong please." I began to cry.

Clyde looked me in my eyes. "Baby I'm not going to lie to you. I promised lil Meth that I would not tell you but baby I have too now. About three weeks ago I came home early, and junior was home. I asked him what happened why he wasn't in school and he said he played hooky today. I asked him why and he told me he owed this guy some money. I looked at him and said what do you mean? He said he was selling weed in school to people and the guy

53

that put him on wanted his money back. He said he spent it on a gift for a girl. So, I had to give the money to the guy, and I told the dude not to ever give my son anything else to sell again or I was going to kill him. I had a long talk with junior and he wants to be a hustler. I told him about everything, and I promised him that it's not the life he wants. He said that he was going to do it anyway. Today when you saw the package it wasn't drugs it really was a gift for you. He went out this morning to pick it up for me. See if I keep him busy, he won't think about hustling. So, Baby you don't have anything to worry about. I am trying to guide him in the right direction."

I sat up and gave him a kiss and told him thank you.

"So, what surprise do you have for me? "With a big smile on his face he said, "You just have to wait and see!"

Chapter Eight
Mee-Mee

"Hello"

"Hey baby girl, how are you?"

"Hi, umm, I have been thinking about you lately and I wanted to know if you missed me and if you do then why haven't you tried to contact me or Meth in so many years?"

My heart was racing when I said all of that and I was feeling like I was going to lose my breath.

"Mee-Mee daddy doesn't have an excuse. I know that your mother had moved on with her life and Clyde took great care of you and your brother. I didn't want to interfere with yall new happy life. I am sorry baby for not being there. I was wrong but I do love you with all my heart you are my baby girl."

"I can't understand right now but maybe one day I will, but I was hoping that we could get to know each other. Can I give you my cell phone number and you call me sometimes? I would like for you to become involved in my life."

Lynaia Jordan

"Sure baby, you can call me anytime. I am always available, and I would like for you to call ya little brother sometimes too. He really wants to get to know you and lil Meth too."

"Ok, that will be cool for me but lil Meth is a different story. I will send you a picture of me."

"I will send you one too, Alright I love you baby and can't wait to see you. Let me know if you want to come and see me, I will get you here and back home safely."

I started to laugh, and then I said "ok, see you soon."

When I hung the phone up with him, I felt so much better in the inside. It was great to hear his voice. I really do want to get to know him. I wonder if he looks the same from the picture, I have in my dresser draw. As I walked towards the living room, I overheard junior's phone conversation. I couldn't believe what he was saying I have to tell mother. I walked to my mother's room door when I saw her and Clyde talking. She was crying. I don't know but for some reason I think it has something to do with lil Meth. I will keep my mouth close for now but if my mother gets hurt, I am going to hurt somebody. I walked in my room so that I could take a good picture to send my father but first I have to call my best friend Connie and let her know what I just did.
"Connie what are you doing?"

Lynaia Jordan

"Nuffin Mee what's up?"

"Well I just talked to my father, the one that lives in Baltimore. I told him how I felt, and it felt good too, He said that he thought we had a happy family with Clyde, so he tried to give my ma's her space, but he misses us though. My moms got us some tickets to go to Baltimore in like a month so that we could see him."

"So, Mee, what do Meth think about going to see ya father?"

"On da real he doesn't know but he aint gonna want to see him you know better than anyone the only person he can talk to is Clyde."

"Are you gonna tell him that yall going?"
"No, my mom's gonna tell him you know we still not speaking."

"Girl you really need to get over that, he is ya brother, but he is fine as hell and if we talk then you can't be mad."

"Yes, I can Connie and if you were a real friend you would have told him you can't talk to him."

"Well Mee-Mee I am a real friend that's why I told you. I have feeling for ya brother and he wouldn't do anything to hurt you so I know he wouldn't do anything to hurt me. Do you wanna go to the mall with us today so we can talk?"

"No, I have to practice for my audition next week for the dance school. I will hit you when I'm done."

"Ard then, I will come pass after we come from the mall."

"Ard girl talk to you later."

"See you later Mee girl!"

I flopped back on my bed and just pictured my father's face. I really miss him. Sometime my mother would tell me stories of how he would talk to me in a baby voice and call me his little
princess. I took two pictures and sent to his phone. I waited for like five minutes to get a response, but nothing ever came through. Maybe he is on the phone or it's dead. Whatever it is I know he will respond. That's when Clyde walked in the room.

"Hey Mee baby, do you want to go to the mall with me and
junior?"

"No sir, I am going to stay here with mommy and practice my routine."

Lynaia Jordan

"Ard baby girl, do you want me to pick you up anything?"

"No thanks, I will be ok for now."

"Ok see you later."

He closed the door. I jumped up off my bed and begin to dance in the mirror. I loved to watch myself dance. I could do pretty much any kind of dance. I was the bomb and I knew it! As I looked at myself in the mirror, I didn't see that little girl anymore I saw a little woman developing and I loved what I saw. While I was in the mirror dancing, I didn't realize my mother was standing in the door way watching me.

"Mee-Mee" I turned around fast like she could read my thoughts.

"Yes"

"Do you wanna ride with me to Wal-Mart; I need to get a
couple of things?"

"No, I'm gonna take my daily walk. I'm ok, but ma if you see some cute shorts can you picks me up a pair?"

"Yeah girl, you should have gone to the mall with junior and

59

Lynaia Jordan

Clyde."

"I know but I didn't want to miss my daily workout. I am
getting myself in this habit because when I get into this school I am going to have to be in shape."

I put up my muscles to her and began to laugh.

"Well ok I will see you later baby. Keep your phone charged
just in case I see something I can text a picture to you."

"Ok ma talks to you later."

She closed the door behind her, and I looked in the mirror one more time before I put my walking clothes on. I was all ready to go when my cell phone rung. I didn't know the number, so I didn't answer it. I was thinking maybe they will leave a voice message. They didn't so I started my walk, by time I got to the bottom of the driveway I felt my phone vibrate I had a text message. It read

I have been watching you for a while, I asked your best friend if you had a boyfriend and she told me no. So, I wanted to know if you wanted to go to the last school dance with me?

Once I read the text message, I called the number back. "Hello, did someone call Mee-Mee?"

Lynaia Jordan

"Yeah is this Mee-Mee"

"This is Allen from ya math class. I'm for texting you but I am a little shy and I didn't know how you would react if I called ya phone. Your best friend gave me your number so I could ask you to the dance."

OMG, this is Allen, curly hair, light skinned Allen. Ok, Mee get yourself together, just tell him ok, you will go to the dance with him.

"Oh, Allen, hey. Well I don't have a date for the dance, and I would love to go with you. I'm about to go for my walk so I will hit you after I come back is this your number?"

"Yes, this is my number. I can't wait to hear from you later."
When he hung up the phone, I couldn't wait to call Connie.

"Connie, why in the hell you didn't tell me that you gave fine ass Allen my phone number?"

Connie laughed in my ear before she said, "Girl that was a month ago, I forgot anyway because he was talking all fast and I was trying to make it to practice so I forgot to tell you but anyway what did he say?"

Lynaia Jordan

"Girl he asked me to the dance, and he said he wanted me to call him back later. He is the cutest guy in the school!"

"Girl please, meth is the cutest in the school. "We both laughed.

"Well ok that's all I wanted to say I will see you later. I am going to call him when you get here so we can laugh at how shy he is."

"Ard Mee see you later."

I walked and thought about Allen the whole time. Allen is a light skinned, curly hair boy who is the Capitan of the school's basketball team. Every girl in the school wants him. He was adopted by his aunt when his parents died in a fire. He is so
cute, we gonna look good together.

I returned back to the house. I see that my mother or Clyde wasn't home yet, so I took a shower and got ready for dinner.

Once I put my close on, I grabbed my phone and see that I had one missed call from a number in Baltimore. I thought that it was my father, so I checked my voicemail. To my surprise it
was my little brother.

Lynaia Jordan

Hello, hello maybe this is her voicemail. Hi, this is Melik your little brother I was calling you to give you my phone number and I am going to send you a picture of me. I can't wait to see you Mee. Daddy sent me a picture of you, and you are very pretty you look just like your mother she is beautiful too. I can't wait to meet yall. Hope to talk to you soon. Bye.

I just sat on my bed at first, thinking about what he said. Daddy, wow that would be a big step for me to call meth daddy. Any way let me look at this picture. When I opened up the text from him, I couldn't believe my eyes. He looks just like lil Meth except he is a little taller and thicker. I have to show this picture to my mother. When she came home, we were the only two in the house at first, so I pulled out my phone and told her to look.

My mother jaws dropped. "Mee who is this?"

"Ma it is Melik my little brother."

"Wow, he and junior looks just alike."

"I know Ma; I think Junior is going to be mad." Just when I said that Junior, Clyde and Connie walked in the kitchen.

"What now Mee, what am I going to be mad about?"

Lynaia Jordan

"Look nothing Junior, you know I have nothing to say to you so don't start speaking and talking to me now."

I turned around and walked to the living room, I didn't feel Junior come up behind me.

"Look Mee. I love you and I know that I should not have talked to Connie, but we talk now so, and I really got mad love for her. Mee if you want me to stop talking to her I will. I hate when you feel upset."

I stood there and looked him in his eyes, and I knew he was telling me the truth.

"I don't want you to do that Junior I just wanted yall to apologize to me for going behind my back. I love both of yall. Since you just apologized it's cool for yall to talk but the first time yall decide to leave each other alone don't try to talk bad about each other around me. Agreed?"

"Agreed sis."

We gave each other a hug and then I looked over at Connie and said "Agreed Connie"

"Yeah Mee, Agreed."

We sat at the table and began to eat like a family, when my mother started up a conversation.

Lynaia Jordan

"Hey Mee, how was your walk today?"

"Ma it was cool, I received a phone call and got asked to the school dance."

Junior and Clyde looked at me.

Junior said, "Bye who?"

"Well since you must know it was Allen."

Clyde asked Junior "Who is this clown Allen?"
"He is the captain of the basketball team. He is a cool dude stay to his self, got a little part time job at Kroger's like three days a week. No brother or sister and live over on Duncan lane with his aunt."

"Dag Junior you know everything about him. You get on my nerves, yall don't have to do that with me. I don't get in you and Connie business so don't get in mines."

"Chill baby girl he just was answering my question. You know I have to protect my princess. "Clyde gave me a little grin.

"Well anyway I told him I would go so I need to get a dress and things for the dance."

My mother interrupted me and said "On a different note, I would like take a family vote on a family trip. I

Lynaia Jordan

would like to attend my class reunion in Baltimore, and I would like for everyone to come so we could see our family and old friends. Majority vote will be the ruling and I won't be upset if yall don't want to go. So, I voted go! Junior voted next and said Stay. Clyde voted and said Go.

My vote was the last one and I voted Go.

"So, it is a go, I will have everything together and ready for us to leave next month."

Junior got up from the table and walked in the living room. My mother got up and went after him.

Lynaia Jordan

Chapter Nine
Junior

Man, I just don't understand why in the hell do she want to go back to Baltimore its nothing there for us.

"Junior, what's wrong son?"

I looked up into my mother's eyes and I though it is time to tell her how I really feel about Baltimore and my father.

"Ma sit down please. Ma, I don't want to go to Baltimore, I feel like it's nothing there for us. We have a great family here; nice friends and we are surrounded around good people. In Baltimore all the stories I heard was about you are getting hurt ma. I swear if someone tries to hurt you now, I will kill them. My father abandoned us for another family. He didn't really love us. He came here because he knew how good Clyde was treating you. He didn't want us, he just wanted you. He doesn't call or anything. I hate him Ma."

"Junior, don't say that. He is still your father and I asked him to stay away. I was the selfish one; I was hurt so I left. This
house that we live in, he brought for us. I don't agree with every decision your father made in life but it's one thing I

know for sure is that he loves you and Mee Mee. He has respected my wishes and left our family alone. He came here and saw how happy yall was with Clyde and he just wanted yall to continue to be happy. Junior your father has been talking to Mee-Mee. I am letting you know that it is your decision whether you want him in your life. But I am also saying if I was you, I would give him a chance he really is a great guy. Junior I love you so much and would never to do anything to hurt you, you and Mee-Mee are my world, my everything."

Looking into my mom's face I know that she really means everything she says. She gave me hug and assured me that everything is going to be ok. My mother is a strong woman and when I grow up, I want for my wife to be just like her. I am going to go to Baltimore, but I am not going to act like I am happy about Meth. Not at all. I walked up to Mee-Mee and let her know that we need to talk later.

"Ok Junior, I got you."

We ate dinner and watched a movie and got thing together for church in the morning. My mom took Connie home; Clyde wanted to ride with her to give me and Mee-Mee sometime to talk. Clyde sees and hears everything.

"Hey Mee, are you ready to talk?"

"Yeah what's up?"

Lynaia Jordan

"Well first I want to know why you aint tell me that you have been talking to Methon?"

"Look Junior, I know how you feel about him, so I didn't see the need to try and convince you that he was cool."

"Ok, now I want your honest opinion about him."

"Honestly Junior, I think he is cool. Ma asked him to stay away and he did. He just wanted what was best for us. We got a little brother and he would like for all of us to get to know each other a little better."

"Ok, so what does this little brother looks like?"

"Look I have a picture of him on my phone."

I grabbed her phone and when I saw this big ass youngin I was mad. This nigga looks just like me.

"He looks like me, yeah he my little brother. So now what have you been talking to him too?"

"Naw, I haven't called him back yet, I just got his message
tonight, before yall came back home."

"Well call him I want to hear this nigga's voice."

Lynaia Jordan

The phone rang twice then he picked up "hello."

"Mee-Mee said "Hello, umm can I speak to Melik?"

"Yeah this is Melik. How are you?"

"You know who this is?"

"Yes, this is my big sister Meshun, aka Mee-Mee." He laughed.

"Hey Melik, you right this is Mee-Mee, but I have our big brother on the phone to Junior."

"What's up Junior?"

"What's up Melik."

"I'm glad yall called me, I have wanted to talk to yall for a long time, but Dad keep telling me it wasn't the right time. I was shocked when he came in my room and told me it was the right time."

"So Melik, you and Methon live together?"

"Yup, my whole life. I never lived with my mother. Our dad is my best friend. He really is great you know; I can't wait until we can get to know each other. When are yall coming up here?"

"In like a month, our mother is coming too. Do your mother live with yall?"

"Well no, she has her own house, but she is over a lot. I don't want to talk no more over the phone I want yall to come here. It is so many people yall need to meet, Ria, lil Cory he is my best friend even though he is older, granny, that is lil Cory's grandmother, Earl he is my oldest brother. So many people. Yall gonna love it we gonna have some fun."

"Oh really" said Junior. 'Well we will see you in like a month, can't wait keep in touch ard."

"Ok, I love yall, goodbye."

Me and Mee-Mee said goodbye at the same time. I looked at Mee-Mee and we both started to laugh. He sounded country and young.

"Look sis, I'm going up here, but I am not going to be chilling with them like that. I just can't see it happening."

"Ok, that's on you I am going to find out information about our family and meet some of Methon's relatives. I want to see grandma, and big pop. I miss them. I want to see Clyde's mom too. But first I have to get this dance out the way."

Lynaia Jordan

Mee-Mee had a huge smile on her face when she said that.

"I don't know why you are smiling he can't touch you!"

She didn't think that was funny, she put me out her room. I was laughing at her when she was telling me to get out. The whole night all I could think about was Baltimore and meeting Meth after all this time. Wondering if I and he look alike. The next morning, I had to talk to Clyde about this.

"Hey Clyde, can I talk to you for a minute?"

"Of course, you can Junior, what is going on with ya?"

"I am so confused on this Methon and Baltimore thing. I have a father and his name is Clyde. You are the person all my friends
know. You come to all my games; you help me with the girl situation. I am scared for real. I don't know how to take him. I am dame sure not letting him come in and take your place. I'm mad at this nigga for taking care of his other kids and just leaving me and Mee-Mee out."

"Well Junior, he sends your mother money for yall every month. She has it in an account waiting for both of yall. That bank card you have it's the money your father sends for yall. He has been sending it for the past ten years.

72

Lynaia Jordan

Check this out Junior, when it comes down to you and Mee-Mee, Meth wants to be a part of yall life but since he has respect for your mother's wishes he stays away. Your mother wanted yall to be old enough to understand the things her and your father went through so yall can make your own decision on how to deal with him. To me he is not a bad guy he just didn't treat your mother how I treat her. That still don't mean he didn't love her, I don't know about all that, and don't care, I just want yall to be good. Knowing you Junior you gonna make the right decision, you always do!"

See this is why I always come to Clyde he is straight up with me and he knows just what to say.

"Thanks Clyde, you really helped me a lot."

"No thanks needed. I love you man!"

"I love you too!"

Time flew before I knew it, it was the night of the dance. Around my house this was all the talk about. It seemed like we were going to a prom or something. I didn't want so much attention. I decide to just wear a button up shirt and a pair of tennis. I don't know but the only thing that has been on my mind is seeing my father for the first time in like ten years. I am mad for real because he chose to not be a part of our lives and for sure this weekend, I am going to tell him how I feel.

Lynaia Jordan

When I walked past Mee-Mee door I saw her in the mirror smiling at her. When she turned around all I saw was our mother's face. Mee-Mee is really growing up to look just like mommy.

"Hey Mee, you look beautiful. I'm glad you don't look all trashy cause some of these chic's gonna look whack tonight."

She began to laugh.

"Thinks Junior, I try to keep it 100 and classy. I want to make a statement tonight as well. This is our last function at this school and it's gonna be a transition. I just want to make this a cool night to remember."

"Yeah you right sis. I just have so much on my min."

"Like what Junior talk to me?"

"Well for starters I can't stop thinking about Meth. For real I am so mad at him, he left us and raised his other child. That's what really hurting me the most."

"Junior, let that shit go for real. We are blessed to have a wonderful mother and father. Meth is going to have to live with his decisions. Clyde has been our father since birth for real. He loves us so much. It doesn't matter what meth does and say Clyde is our father. You just be thankful that we had him in our life. Give Meth a chance though you never know what his situations was like back then. Just give him a chance ok."

She walked over and gave me a hug and told me I was good, and she loved me.

"Come on with that sweet stuff man now I am going to smell
fruity."

We both started to laugh and headed down the steps. Our mother was standing in the living room with a camera and tears in her eyes.

"Wow, you guys look great. Don't they Clyde?"

He stood up off the couch and looked us both over.

"Yeah they look alright." With a smirk on his face.

"Come on Clyde we have to hurry, or we are going to be late, you know we have to pick up Allen. Oh, and don't be all in my face at the dance."

"Girl who are you talking to. I am gonna be all in ya grill and you know it!"

We got in the car and headed to Allen's house he came running to the car this boy was mad excited.

Lynaia Jordan

"Mee-Mee you look beautiful, how are you Mr. Clyde and Junior?"

"Hey what's up?"

I looked in the back seat when Allen told Mee-Mee she looked beautiful and her cheeks were red as hell. When we pulled up no one was out front, so I knew it was jumping in the school. I walked through the gym doors and everyone was in my face. I saw my boys over by the DJ table and Connie was talking to her friends. One of them told her I just came in and she turned around and started to walk towards me. She looked cute for real. I don't know that night I wasn't in my right mind my head was somewhere else. The party was jumping, and we had fun. Allen stayed with Mee-Mee the whole night. Everyone was on Mee-Mee though because she looked like a high school girl for real.

Once we left the dance Clyde took us out to eat and then we went home. Saturday morning was here, our flight leaves at 4. I was all packed, but I wasn't ready to go. Clyde came in my room to put my stuff in the car when he asked me if I was ok.

"Naw Clyde, I'm scared, all I know is Georgia. I wish you were our father."

Lynaia Jordan

"Come on son I am your father, just chill you gonna be good, I will be there with you every step of the way I promise."

He gave me a hug and then we walked the bags to the car. The fight was two hours long, I looked over at my mother and she looked scared, Clyde looked ready and Mee-Mee looked excited. I feel asleep on the plane and the next thing I know we were landing at BWI.

Chapter Ten
Sun

When we landed in Baltimore I was scared. Was I ready to face my past? Have I grown enough to face what I have been hiding from the past ten years? We rented two cars so that Clyde and I can both have ways to get around up here. We are staying at his mother's house since she has enough room for all of us.

"Come on Mee and Junior we need to get these bags in the car."

"I want to ride with Clyde Mee-Mee said."

"Ok, Junior can ride with me."

This will give us a chance to talk. I have noticed the past month he has been in deep though, and hardly talking. Once we got on 295, I knew it was almost show time.

"Ma, can I ask you a question."

"Sure Junior, what is it?"

"Well, ma can you tell me what really happened between you and Meth and why he stayed away. I just don't understand. Did you love him? Did he love us? Who is my brothers' mother? Did she play a part in the reason why yall broke up?"

"Wait a second junior one question at a time. Well first thing is yes, I loved your father and yes, he loved us. Second sometimes when you are young you make the wrong decisions. Your brother mother had a lot to do with it, but it was also mine and your fathers' decision. Our love just wasn't strong enough to make it last that's all. Meth has changed his self a whole lot and he is not the little boy I fell in love with a long time ago. He is a different man now.

Junior I just want you to give him a chance to make things right with you. You know when you came down the steps Wednesday night with your sister all I saw was me and your father. You look just like him. You act like me a little, but you are his son. So, I will always have a soft spot in my heart for your father because I have you."

For the rest of the ride Junior was quiet and I think he understood now. I have to talk to Meth before he talks to the kids. This is what I didn't want but we have to see each other one day. When we arrived at Clyde's Mother house, she was standing outside waiting for us to pull up. She really missed us and the kids.

Once we got settled in, I told Clyde and the kids I wanted to go and see my mother and Ria. Clyde said he would drive too because he had a couple of things, he needed to pick up so after we seem my mother he would go and take of it. I wasn't sure what he was talking about, but I just let him be.

The kids were so excited they haven't seen my mother in a while. When we pulled up, it brought back so many memories, of me and Meth. Before I could even ring the doorbell, my little sister Joy came running out hugging them and kissing them. I was laughing because she really missed us. Once she finished with the kids, she came to me and Clyde. We hugged for like five minutes I really miss her nagging tail.

"Where is mommy?"

"This early, she better gets up."
"She is up in her bedroom in the be."

I yelled up the steps
"Ma come on down here, the kids want you"

"Sun, I need to talk to you come in the kitchen."

I got this cramp in my stomach as I walked in the kitchen. Joy turned and looked at me and said

"Mommy is sick she has to have an operation next month and they are hoping that everything workout ok."

"Joy what kind of sick and why didn't you call me and let me know?"

Lynaia Jordan

"Mommy told me to promise her I wouldn't tell you because she didn't want you to worry."

"Well Joy what's wrong with her?"

"She has cancer. She was in remission, but she didn't have the surgery she has to have a liver transplant. She is on the
waiting list and it might come up with in a month."

"Oh my god, you didn't call me."

I began to cry then I walked up the steps to my mother's room. The kids and Clyde were already up there with her. I walked in the room and everyone turned to face me. I have a feeling that Clyde already knew but this is not the time or place to ask him.

"Hey ma."

"Hey Sun, come here and give me a hug."

My mother doesn't even look like herself, she looks really sick, but I know God is a good God and he will bring my mother
through this.

"Hey kids won't yall go downstairs with Joy so I can talk to
grandma for a minute."

81

Lynaia Jordan

Once the kids and Clyde left out the room I turned to my mother with tears in my eyes and said, "Ma why didn't you tell me, you know I would have come home to help you."

"I know baby, but I didn't want to worry you. You were getting your life together and raising them beautiful babies of yours. Sun, Junior looks just like Meth. Have he seen them yet?"

"Ma, I don't want to talk about Meth I want to talk about you and how I am here until after the surgery. Whatever you need I am here. I am so mad at you ma."

"Sun please don't be mad at me. I just didn't want you to
worry, but everything is going to be ok. The transplant will get done and I will be back two normal in like two months."

"Ok ma but until then, I am here. I am not going anywhere."

Me and my mother talked for like an hour then I told her I was going to take the kids to see Ria. Before we left my mother house, I had to talk to Clyde, so we took a walk to the park around the corner and talked. When we got to the park, I turned to him and broke down all he could do was hold me and tell me that everything would be ok.

Lynaia Jordan

In a sobbing voice I got out "Clyde I am so scared I don't want to lose my mother; she is everything to me, I am so tired of losing everyone I love Clyde."

He just stood there and held me then lifting my head up off his shoulder he said, "Sun, we can stay for as long as you like. My family have plenty of room for us, your mother needs you."

I kissed him and let him know he is the best. I love my husband and I know he loves me. I have to tell the kids. As we walked back to the house, he held my hand and just keep saying "Baby you re strong and you are going to make it though, your mother is going to be ok."

"Come on kids lets go see ya cousin Ria and talk, I need to tell yall something."

I ran upstairs to tell my mother we would be back later, and I will bring her some soup in for dinner. Once we got in the car, I told the kids what's was about to happen and how we were going to stay here for the whole summer. Mee-Mee was excited, but Junior had a look of disappointment on his face. Pulling up in front of Ria's salon brought back memories when I was in labor.

"Hey, do yall know I went in labor with yall sitting right here in front of ya cousin's salon."
They both looked at each other and started to laugh.

Lynaia Jordan

"Come on let's go in."

"What in the world, I know it's not my little cousins?"

"Yes, it is this is Mee-Mee and Junior."

"Well come here yall and give cousin Ria a hug, I haven't held yall since yall were babies."

"Ria, it really looks good in here, I see you have a kiddie spa added onto the salon now."

"Yeah Sun it has come a long way in ten years, girl it's been
hard but I have been doing ok, I can't complain. So, have you
talked to Meth yet?"

"No, he doesn't know we are here, I was going to stop past the Car Wash next."

"He might be ready to leave in a few minutes wont I call him, and we could go out to dinner so that Melik can meet yall?"

I looked at the kids and they both said "ok"

"Let me take my mother some soup and we will meet you in an hour at the Applebee's."

"Cool I will call Meth and let him know, I am almost done my last client, it sure is good to see you Sun."

"It's good to see you to Ria."

I called Clyde to let him what we were going to do, and he was cool with it. "Baby I will just see you and the kids later tonight. I love yall so much."

"I love you to baby."

I stopped past Safeway and got so soup for my mother. When I walked through the door, I surprised to see Meth sitting on the chair talking to Joy. I hurried and walked to the kitchen because I wasn't ready to see him or talk to him yet. I had to pump myself up. I could smell him coming behind me in the kitchen. I took a deep breath and turned around to have him standing right in my face. He looked so good his eyes, his face, his hair. We just stood there and looked at each other for like a minute until we heard Mee-Mee clearing her throat. Meth turned around to see who it was.

"Hey baby girl, how are you?"

"Hey, I'm ok."

"Well come and give ya father a hug."

Lynaia Jordan

When she walked to him, she was smiling so hard. I could hear her whisper in his ear "I knew you looked like this, I missed you daddy."

Meth squeezed her tight and said, "I missed you too baby girl."

When he looked up, he saw Junior standing there.

"Man, you are big, and you got a nice-looking face too."

Meth was trying to be funny, but Junior didn't laugh he just stared at him. I saw tears in Juniors eyes, so I broke the ice.

"So are yall ready to go eat?"

Mee-Mee jumped right in the middle, "Yes ma, I am starving."

We started to walk to the door, When I heard Meth say, "Hey Junior could you ride with me?"

I was standing there waiting for junior to say no but I was in shock when ok came out his mouth.

"Ok, let me get my phone out the car."
When junior walked to the car, I smiled at Meth. He knew I was so happy junior was going to ride with him.

Lynaia Jordan

"We are going to meet yall at the restaurant."

Once in the car Mee-Mee decided to start a conversation with me.

"So, ma, I saw how you were staring at my father."

I hurried and turned my head to her and said 'What" I laughed a little then said "Look Mee-Mee whatever I and your father had for each other is over. I love your dad! Clyde!"

I looked at Mee-Mee and then we both laughed.

"Look ma I know that you love Clyde but if you could have seen the way you and my father was looking at each other just now. It was like Snow White getting woke by her prince charming kiss."

"Sometimes Mee-Mee looks can be deceiving."

"Ok, I won't mention the look again, but I am just letting you know that I know what I saw."

"Now since when you became an expert on love and looks, you better be an expert on Math, and Reading I know that. Honestly sweetheart, me and your father is over, he has moved on and so have I. We are still friends and will always be that no matter what."

87

Lynaia Jordan

Mee-Mee took me back to the look, I knew deep down inside I still felt something for Meth it never left really, I just tucked it away because it was the best thing for me to do. I could remember when he would hold me and just look me in my eyes and tell me how much he loved me, and I was his heart. Once we pulled up to the restaurant Meth and Junior was already standing in the parking garage waiting for us. This is going to be an interesting night.

Lynaia Jordan

Chapter Eleven
Meth

I know that this is going to be an interesting summer. finding out that Sun is staying up here the whole summer. This gives me enough time to try and win my family back. I am not going to stop at nothing to have back my family.

"So Junior, do you like to play sports?"

"Yeah, I like to play football."

"Are you any good?"

"I do ok, I'm not the team superstar but I do ok. I hope one day to be an NFL Player."

"Well son if you put your mind to it you can do anything."

"Umm, Meth you can call me Junior."

I heard the tone in his voice change; I know that he has something on his chest. I deal with Melik all the time and I need to get this addressed right now.

"So, Junior, do you have anything you want to talk to me about or need to talk to me about?"

At first, he gave me a look then he said

Lynaia Jordan

"Yeah, I do. I have a lot of question to ask you. Starting with why you left your family to start another one?"

"Junior it's a long story."

"Well Meth it seems like I got the whole summer to listen!"

"Ok son, I will start tomorrow let's eat dinner with ya mother and sister. I will come and pick you up in the morning and you can spend the whole day with me. I will tell you everything."

"Ard, I will be ready."

I was starving and I couldn't wait to sit down and have a meal with my family. I really miss my heart. She got a little older, but she is still as beautiful as the first time I saw her. My baby girl looks just like her except she has my eyes.

"Come on Junior lets go and open up the doors for your mother and sister."

"Man, I'm not doing that, they not handy cap."

He was laughing the whole time saying those words. When junior smiled it looked like I was looking in the mirror. I missed out on everything with my son. I snapped out my deep thought when Sun got out the car.

"Hey Meth, is Ria still meeting us here?"

Lynaia Jordan

"Yeah, I think so, she gonna call me when she is on her way,
You know her if she said she coming she is."

"Yeah you right."

"Sun is Clyde coming?"

She turned her head to look at me so fast. "No, Methon he is not, Is Peaches coming?"

I laughed a little then said "Naw I told her to stay home tonight but I would like for all of yall to come past the house after dinner to meet Melik and Lil Cory."

"Oh my god Meth, I haven't heard that name in a long time."

I looked over at Sun and she had tears in her eyes.

"Hey, are you ok?"

"Yeah Meth I'm good, it just has been a long time, too long!
How old is Lil Cory now?"

"He will be 16 in a couple of months. He is a good boy Sun he doesn't give his grandmother no trouble. He would really love to see you; he still has your picture up on his wall."

"I truly missed him; I wish that I could have taken him with me when I moved but I didn't want to do that to his grandmother."

"He knows that Sun."

We walked into the restaurant together and it was a section closed off for us. I knew the twins was going to be surprised when they saw the section. I had a banner hanging on the wall Welcome Home Twins!

"Thanks Meth this is nice." Said Mee-Mee
Junior only looked and didn't say a word. When we sat at the table everyone was quiet, so I decided to start a conversation.

"Hey Sun, tomorrow do you want to go and see Lil Cory and the kids could meet their brother Melik?"

"Um, I don't see why not it would be ok with me. Is that ok twins?"

Mee-Mee was right on board. "Yup, cool with me." But Junior had to be the one. "Well I have to see if Clyde has anything planned for me for tomorrow. I will let you know after I check with him."

Lynaia Jordan

I kind of thought that the little talk we had in the car made a difference in how he feels about me, but I guess it didn't. The waitress came over to our table and started to take our order when she got to Sun, she stopped and looked hard.

"Excuse me miss but did you use to live in Flaghouse Projects?"

Sun looked up at her and said, "Yeah Why?"

"Sun it's me Penny. Little Penny that lived in 127 Building on the 10th floor."

"Oh, hey girl, you have grown up, you not little Penny any
more."

"Yeah, I am in college now, this is my last year. I have been trying to find you for a while. My grandmother passed and I really wanted to thank you for looking out for me back in the day."

"Oh, Penny girl it was nothing, I would have done it for anyone."
While Sun and the waitress talked and exchanged numbers I just sat there and looked at her. This was one of the reasons why I loved this woman so much.
"Meth, Meth!"

Lynaia Jordan

I felt Mee-Mee shake my arm and I came out of my daze. "Sorry baby girl, yeah what's up?"

"Well what I wanted to know was why were you staring at
 mommy like that?"

I laughed and little then said "What are you talking about I was looking at the salt shaker. "

That was the first thing that came to my mind. We both laughed but once again Junior didn't find anything funny.

"So, twins what do yall want from the menu?"

"Well since ladies are first, I would like to have some crab dip and an order of buffalo wings with a side of fries."

"Dang, Mee you must be hungry." Said Junior.

"Well I am, it's different here, moms always cook dinner and we always eat at a certain time. I'm just saying I have to get use to this for the rest of the summer."

The next morning, I called Sun to ask her if she wanted to go today to see little Cory and she agreed.

"Sun, could I come and pick yall up that way we could just ride together?"

"Meth that's not a good idea we will meet you at Lil Cory's grandmother's house."

Lynaia Jordan

"Ok, Sun I will meet you there then could we go back to my place so the kids can meet Melik?"

"Meth I will see."

When she hung up, I knew that Sun had feelings about me having a child with Peaches, but she really needs to get over it. Melik is my son and I am not going to choose between my family and my son.

Chapter Twelve
SUN

Once I found out that my mother was sick, I decided to stay at her house for the summer. I really didn't want to leave her side and Joy said that it makes her happy to see me and the kids around all the time.

"Ma, can I talk to you for a second?"

"Sure Sun" Ms. Brownstone sat up on her bed to let Sun she had her undivided attention.

"Well, Meth asked me if I would let the kids go and meet Melik. I didn't say anything ma because I still have feelings about that. That is Peaches son and she did a lot of hurtful and hateful things to me ma. Do you think I am carrying it wrong?"

"Baby listen, you have a right to be mad at Peaches but not Melik. Sun, I met him, he is a very sweet young man. Meth is raising him the right way Sun."

"You are right Ma, but the first time he asks me to meet Peaches it going to be on."

I looked my mother straight in her face and we both started to laugh. I gave her a hug and told her I loved her.

Lynaia Jordan

"Oh man, did you need me to do anything before I leave out?"

"No baby you just go and enjoy yourself. I will be right here when you get back."

The kids were already in the car waiting and I was nervous because I really didn't want to meet him, but I know the kids did. When we pulled up at Lil Cory's grandmothers house Meth was already there waiting. He smiled when he seen me get out the car. The twins got out the car and began to walk towards Meth. Mee-Mee gave him a hug and junior gave him a look.   Meth   broke the ice and said, "Hey kids, yall ready to meet yall god brother?"

"Yeah I'm ready." Said Mee-Mee

Once again Junior just gave him a look. I didn't say anything because I wanted to see how long he was going to act like this. When meth opened the door, Cory's mother was sitting in the
living room waiting on us.

"Hey ma, they are here."

"Oh, my come here baby you look just like your mother when she was younger, and you junior, you look just

like ya dad. I mean he spit you out. Sun come here sweetie, you are still
beautiful." said Cory's mother.

I walked over to the couch and gave her a kiss her kiss on her cheek. She still looks mean, but I know she was a very nice woman.

"So where is lil Cory?" Mee-Mee asked

"Baby he should be in here any minute. He ran to the store to get me a Pepsi."

Just then the door opened, and this handsome young man came walking through the door. I thought I was looking at Ruby with a Cory complexion and height. I have seen pictures of him, but I didn't know seeing him would tear me up so much inside.

"Hey Gramps, the Pepsi's wasn't cold. I got it anyway. Did you want some ice in a glass? Oh, and hello everyone." Lil Cory said with a smile on his face.

I stood up and walked to him and touched his face. I hugged him so tight. I just could stop the tears from flowing from my face.

"I love you so much. I am so sorry for leaving you. I thought it was best for you to be here with your grandmother. I was young. You were the best thing that happened to me." I whispered in his ear. I lifted my head up and introduced him to Mee- Mee and Junior.

Junior gave him a head nod and said, "What's up."

Mee-Mee said "Hello"

"Well are you guys ready to go pick up Melik and then hit the amusement park?"

"Yup" said Mee-Mee.

I gave him a look because I didn't tell him if I was ready to meet him or not.

"See you later, we will bring lil Cory back a little later." Meth said to lil Cory's grandmother

"Umm Meth can I talk to you for a second?"
We walked out to my car and the kids got in his car.

"Yeah Sun what's up?"

"Meth I didn't tell you I was going to play motherfucking family with you and your son. I never answered and quite frankly I don't think that I am ready for that. You cheated on me with his mother time and time again. You hurt my heart Meth. How do you think I am supposed to feel? I just don't know."

Lynaia Jordan

"Are you finish?"

"Yeah!"

"Sun baby I am so sorry for hurting you. I love you but I am not going to tell you that my son is not going to be a part of your life because his mother is Peaches. I know what she did was wrong, but my son had nothing to do with that. If you want to be mad at someone be mad at me. What I can't take is you being this cold person. I don't know this woman. You were so strong, even when you were hurt. I will not choose between my kids anymore. I beg you please don't disrespect me or yourself by acting this way with my son."

He looked me in the eyes and then walked to the car. I stood there for a second trying to get my head together because he was right. I got in my car and followed Meth to his house.

When we pulled up, I remember pulling up here before I left and whipping Peaches ass after she had the baby. She deserved it. I had to take a few breaths before I got out the car cause if she was here, I might go the fuck off. We didn't even get out the car and he ran out the house towards the car. He looked just like Peaches, had Meth complexion though. I got out the car and walked towards Meth and the kids. He came up to me and gave me a hug.

"Hello Ms. Sun, I am Melik, I am so glad I finally get to meet the woman that has my dad's heart."

I smiled a little then said "Oh yeah he definitely been around
you too long."

"Like father like Son." Meth said

When he said that Junior walked away.

"Junior" I called him

He began to run and that's when Meth ran after him. Mee-Mee looked worried then she said, "Well since they wanna do the running let's go inside and have a seat." Mee-Mee looked at Melik and grabbed him by the neck to put him in a head lock. He just laughed. Before I walked into the house, I prayed that I didn't see Peaches because I am not ready for that chapter yet. Melik yelled up the steps and called someone.

"Hey E come down here and meet Ms. Sun and my big sister
Mee-Mee."

We must be one of his friends. We walked and sat in the living room waiting for Meth and Junior to come back. I let Meth go after him because I didn't want him to tell me how he felt. I wanted Meth to hear it. I know that my son is hurting because he doesn't have a relationship with Meth and on top of the fact, he looks just like him. Just then this tall dark-skinned boy came running down the stairs. He walked over lil Cory gave him a five then walked to me and said, "Hello Ms. Sun, I am Earl Peaches oldest son."

My jaws dropped; I never would have thought Meth would have him too. Maybe Meth has turned into a different kind of guy.

"Hello Earl, this is my daughter Mee-Mee she is a twin, Meth went to get her brother Junior. How old are you now Earl?"

"I am sixteen same as lil Cory, I will be graduating next year."

"Well that is good. Are you going to college?"

"Yes, since I came to live with Meth, my life has been better he is the greatest man I ever met."

Wow is he standing here talking about the same man I loved deep down in my heart. Just then Meth and Junior walked through the door.

"Sun could we talk to you for a second."

"Of course, Meth."

Mee-Mee gave Junior a look and he gave her a nod. That was something they did with each other. We walked

Lynaia Jordan

out to Meth's backyard and I was so shocked to see what I saw out there.

Chapter Thirteen
Mee-Mee

Damn, he was super cute. My little brother gotta hook his sister up. I sat there on the chair thinking about Junior and what him and Meth was talking about, but I am going to have to call Connie and tell her about E. Right when I was about to stand up, Meth and Junior walked through the door and asked to talk to mommy. Since they were going to leave out, I decided to sit here with Earl, Lil Cory and Melik to see if I could get a little info on Earl.

"So Melik, I heard that his mother name is Peaches, so is this ya Brother?"

Lil Cory busted out laughing.

"Cory what's so funny?"

"Nuffin"

"Yup, my mother never had him either."

"Damn both of yall talking about me like I aint even standing right here." Earl said.
"Excuse me, I just was trying to get a little info on you. Didn't wanna push up on my half-brother and all."

Lynaia Jordan

He gave me a serious look and walked up the stairs. I watched him, then he stopped and turned around and saw me looking.

"What" I said to him he just shook his head and keep walking up the steps.

"Hey Melik so where is your mother?"

"Oh, she doesn't stay here, and my dad. Um I mean our father told her she need to stay away today because he didn't know how your mother was gonna react if she seen her after all these years. My mother is cool she told daddy ok and just call her if he needed anything."

"Damn, my mom was like that in Baltimore let me find out. What else do you know about my mother?"

He changed the subject fast. It must be some stuff he knows about my mom's, but I will get to the bottom of it.

"Do you play the game like Xbox or PlayStation?" Melik said

"Yes, our brother Junior is the best that ever did it. Do you wanna make a little wager on it?"

"What kind of wager?"

Lynaia Jordan

When he said that Lil Cory went up the steps. I waited for him to get out of our eye site and then I said, "If I beat you hook me up with ya brother."

"Eww Girl that is ya brother too."

"Hell no, he is ya brother, we don't have the same mother or father."

"If daddy heard you, he would get hold to you."

"Well no one is gonna hear me, right?"

Melik gave me a look then said "Yeah sis no one heard you but me. But I'm still not hooking you up!"

We walked up the steps to play the game. I wanted to call Connie to tell her that my brothers' brother was so cute.

"Hey Melik, where is the bathroom?"

"Down the hall on ya right."

"Ard, where the game room at so I could meet you there?"

"It's right here."

"Cool, be back in two." I walked in the bathroom and it was so nice. I must admit my dad did good for his self. His house is beautiful.

"Hey Connie, what you are doing?"

"Missing you and ya brother. How is it up there, and when are yall coming back?"

"Well we will be back when school start causes my grandmother is sick and my mother wanted to be with her. I miss you too, but I need to tell you something and give me ya honest opinion."

"Ok, cool cause I need to ask you something too. So, you go first."

"Ard so my brother Melik has a brother name Earl and Earl is by the lady name Peaches. He sometimes stays with my dad, but he is so cute, and I like him is that a bad thing oh, and he is older?"
"Well yeah cause your father probably look at him like a son. But technically yall not brother and sister so it's not morally wrong."

"Ard cool cause I think I am going to go at him. So, what you need to tell me?"

"I think ya brother is going through something up there. I wanna come up there because he needs me. He called me last night and told me he didn't want to meet yall little brother. He liked it how it was just yall and Clyde. He said that he always wanted Mr. Meth to come in the picture and take care of yall and be with yall but when he didn't, he just let the thought go. Last night yall had dinner, right?"

"Yeah"

"Well after dinner he called me and said that yall mother looked so happy with yall father. He hates the fact that yall father makes her smile like that. It's a lot more but I just want you to keep an eye on him Mee. He needs you to be in his corner. Do you think you can ask ya mother can I come up since yall staying the whole summer?"

"Of course, Connie you got that. I will ask he after he class reunion tonight."

"Ok cool, you know that my mother will say ok, I will just start to get ready. See you soon, love you Mee and call me later and let me know what happened with Earl. He done made you forget all about these boys down here."

I just laughed and hung up. I don't think my mom's gonna let her come up here, but it won't hurt to ask. When I opened up the bathroom door Earl was standing right there.

"Dag what you were listening to me talk?"

Lynaia Jordan

Earl had a look on his face like girl please.

"Nope, just was waiting so I could pee do you mind?"

"No, I don't!" when I walked pass him, I tried to make sure he smelled me.

I walked in the game room and Melik was practicing.

"Melik, how are you going to practice." We both started to laugh. I sat down and picked up the joystick. "Let's play NBA game?"

"Ok, let play, I told my brother that you liked him too."

I punched him "You did what? I didn't say to tell him that. I told you to hook us up." I had a frown on my face when Earl walked in the room. He sat on the coach next to me and said, "Well let me see what you got!"

I smiled a little and told Melik to come on.

"Dag Melik you let a girl whip that ass. You should be ashamed."

"Man, I let her win because she really wanted to win our bet."

Lynaia Jordan

I turned to him so fast. I couldn't believe he just said that. Earl just busted out laughing. I was mad as hell. I got up to go and find mommy and Junior. Before I got to the top of the steps Earl was coming behind me.

"Mee-Mee wait!" he said.

I turned around and he was standing in my face. "I was standing at the bathroom door and I heard what you said to the person on the phone. I think I am a little too old for you, but you are a cutie. On top of that I wouldn't disrespect ya father like that he has been good to me."

I just turned and walked down the steps to find my mother. What do he mean my father? Meth has never been a father to me and furthermore Clyde is my father. I walked out to the back yard to find Junior, my mother and Meth talking by the pool. I think that it is time for me to join the party. As I was walking over to them, I saw Junior wipe his eyes. He must have been crying.

"Hey fam what's up is everyone ready to get going? I wanna have some fun today and every day after that. We met our brother so now it's time to have some fun."

All three of them looked at me and then Meth said "You know what Meshun is right we need to go. Let's go to the waterpark. This is in VA about an hour away yall ready to go?"

Lynaia Jordan

Everyone just started to walk out the door we had two cars, but my father went into the garage. Melik had a surprised look on his face.

"Yo, daddy don't never take this truck out. I mean he don't drive it Nowhere it just sits."

When he pulled out of the garage, he was smiling so hard he had the newest Cadillac Escalade. It was black and beautiful. He pulled up in front of my mother. She gave him a look and then said, "Meth I will drive my own car."

"Sun, we are riding in this truck, I will make sure you make it home safe. Don't make us split up. Everything will be ok."

I was looking my mother in the face and she looked like she wanted ride with him, but she was scared.

She finally said "Ok Meth but were coming back home when I say I'm ready. I know you!"

Meth started to laugh and then said, "Come on kids everyone in the truck."

Junior went straight to the back him, Melik and lil Cory sat back there, Earl sat next to me. I think that Melik did that on purpose. I took a glance at Earl out the corner of my eye and he was so fine.

Lynaia Jordan

Meth looked back at us and said, "Buckle up we are going on the highway."

We all began to laugh because he acted like we were little kids in a car seat or something. He turned the music on, and we began to drive off. I was so worried about starting a conversation with Earl I didn't even hear my phone ring. When I looked down at it, I saw that it was Clyde. I called him back.

"Hello"

"Hey baby girl, how is things going?"

"Well they are ok; we are on our way to the amusement park and then we will be headed back home."

"Oh, where is your mother?"

"Right here, do you want to talk to her?"

"No sweetheart, just keep an eye on her for me, I just want to make sure yall is ok."

"Ok, love you Clyde see you later."

When I hung the phone up Earl was looking right at me. So, I looked back and said "what?"

Lynaia Jordan

He shook his head and said "Aint you a little too young to tell some guy you love them?"

I chuckled, then said "Well since you were all in my conversation I was talking to my stepfather. He is the only man I tell I love you too!"

Oh, my goodness he must like me too cause why would he say that. I want him and I am going to be his girl before the summer is over. I picked my phone up and called Connie because I told her I would call her back and since my mother is singing her songs, I have no one else to talk to. The phone rang twice and no answer I guess she will call me back.   I looked back at Junior and asked him if he talked to Connie. He said "No"

His faced was frowned up a little I wonder why. Then he snapped back and was like "Have you talked to Allen?"

My heart could have dropped because he said Allen name in front of Earl, but I snapped back with the same answer, "No" I turned around fast and looked down at my phone. I got a funny feeling in my stomach, so I am going to keep trying to call Connie. See me and Allen have been talking ever since the dance. He was technically my boyfriend and if I wanna have a chance with Earl I need to break it off with Allen. I don't wanna start off dating as a player. So, I called Allen.

Lynaia Jordan

"Hello"

"Hey Mee, what's up?"

"Nothing just was thinking about you and was wondering what you we're doing?"

"O nothing at the basketball court with a couple of friends. What you are doing?"

"I'm in the car on my way to an amusement park with the fam. So, what's been going on down there." He paused for a second then said, "Nothing much same thing, basketball, swimming and oh Tammy had a party it was hype."

"What Tammy, I know not Tammy over on Peachlife Street?"

"Yup that's the one, she actually asked for you, Connie even went. Well Mee here come my boys I'm gonna hit you tonight. miss you."

"Ok talk to you later and miss you too."

I hung the phone up with confusion because Connie didn't tell me about the party, and we talk about everything.

When we arrived at the Six Flags in Baltimore it was cool but not better than the one, we have in Georgia. I know

Lynaia Jordan

the first thing I wanted to do was eat and then play some games. I really wanted to talk to Connie because I really need to ask her why she didn't tell me about the party. I had to get my mind off of GA and stay focused on what was right here in front of me.

Chapter Fourteen
Sun

Sitting next to him in this car brings back so many memories. I was the shit back then I had everything. We had some good times even though the bad times tore us apart. This is what I pictured our family outing to be minus the step kids. I always knew that me and Meth would be together forever. Only if he could have kept his dick in his pants and left that hoe Peaches alone. I will make the best of this day because this will the closet, he will ever get to having a family with me again.

We pulled up to the park and everyone was ready. Meth was handing out money like he was an atm machine. He told everyone to keep their phones on and hit him if they needed anything. Then he turned and looked at me.

"Well Sun are you rolling with me?"

I looked around at the kids and they were on their way to the gate. "I guess so Meth."

"Ok, you don't have to you know. I could leave you standing right here because you know you aint getting on no rides."

"For your information Mr. I do get on rides"

Lynaia Jordan

"What the tea cup or the water rides?"

"Whatever Meth lets go." We were laughing as we walked to the park entrance.

"Hey Sun, can I ask you a question?"

"Yeah sure."

"Do you miss me?"

"Meth really at the amusement park with the kids. I really don't feel like doing this here so either ask me another question or walk away and enjoy this park by yourself."

"Okay, I'm sorry you know I always have to ask what's on my mind I was looking at you and I miss you that's all."

"Meth I understand that, but this is not the time or the place for this. I came here to have some fun and I will not allow you to turn this into Meth and Sun love reunion."

He looked at me and seen that I was serious, so he busted out laughing at me like he did when we first met. All I could think about was him saying "Damn girl your mouth is ruthless."

Lynaia Jordan

We played a couple of games and of course he had to win me every teddy bear in the park. We decided to go on an indoor roller coaster. I told him he knows I don't do coaster, so he better be prepared to get beat up. We sat down and already he was to close. He had a smirk on his face because how close we were. We began to go inside of the tunnel and then all the lights went out. I then this big ass drops. I was screaming and hugging Meth so tight you would have thought we were one person.

Today I had so much fun with Meth and the kids, but I knew that this fun was going to be over soon. He was only my children's father and not my husband. Even though my heart still skips triple beats when I see him, and he makes me feel like I am still a teenager. The reality is I'm not a teenager any longer. I really need to snap out of this. I love my husband he is wonderful, and he has been there for our children the whole time.

We played all day with the kids at the park, Meth got on every ride with them and I just sat and watched. It was time to go and as we were walking to the car Meth stopped me and suggested to the kids to keep walking.

"Sun, I need to tell you something."

"Ok, what is it?"

Lynaia Jordan

"Well, I know that I have been gone from the kids a long time, but Sun would you consider moving back here so that I could spend some time with them."

"Meth, that is not a decision that I can make alone, I am married, I know that you miss them and everything but taking them from down there to up here is a lot and I just don't think that would be a good idea."

"What if me and the boys move down there by yall. Sun, I need my kids in my life. You may not believe me but if it wasn't for Melik I would have been right down there behind yall."

I pulled my arm away from him and told him "Meth you made your chose now you have to live with the decision."

I began to walk to the car when he ran up and grabbed my arm and said, "Your stubborn woman, I don't care if I die trying, I will get my family back and You will be my queen."

I just keep on walking, but I knew deep down inside he was telling me the truth. So, we made it back home safely and the kids were knocked out, I had to drive out to Clyde's mothers house and then I am going to go and check on my mother. I know she is probably wondering where I am. I called my mother and she said she was fine Clyde and Joy was there and she was in bed I can come past there and be with her tomorrow. I told my mother I loved her, and I would be there in the morning. My phone rung I looked down and it was Meth.

"Hello"

"Sun is it ok if the kids stayed with me tonight?"

"Umm, I have to see if they want to stay." I turned to wake up the twins to ask them

I pulled up to Clyde's mothers house with so much on my mind. I love my husband, don't I? I just keep asking myself that question because of the things that Meth said to me. I just need to take a bubble bath and relax. I need to clear my mind. Music and bubble baths always help. I was laying in the tub of hot water and bubbles listening to my favorite Xscape cd, eyes closed singing. I felt someone standing over top of me. When I opened my it and looked it was my sexy husband. He was naked standing there watching and listening to me. I smiled at him and asked, "Do you want to join me?"

Clyde didn't say a word he just stepped in the tub. He took my feet and began to rub them. He was just looking at me. Then he finally said "Baby are you ok? It looks like something is on ya mind. On top of the fact that you are listening to Xscape."

"Clyde, it is something on my mind. Meth asked me if we could move back up here so he could be close to the kids and if that wasn't an option could he move to Georgia with the boys."

Clyde just paused and looked me in the eyes and said "Baby I love you and our children so much. Nothing and no one will ever come in between that not even Mr. Meth of Baltimore. I will never deny him of seeing his kid, but he will not be a part in raising them. He can be our next-door neighbor he just better knows his place. We are not moving back to Baltimore; you can stay here as long as your mother needs you. Once it's time for the kids to go back to school we will leave for Georgia. Sun, I don't want to talk about Meth anymore. He is not a part of any equation I am in and his wants and needs don't concern me. I love you baby, but I just can't do this with you."

He stood up and got out the tub. When he almost slipped, he turned back and looked at me. That was just what we needed to ease the tension in the room. Clyde was right, Meth wants are not his concern and they shouldn't be mine either. I will keep that stuff to myself so that this won't become an issue for me and my husband. I got out the tub and walked into the bedroom.

Clyde was laying in the bed with the light turned off staring at me. Looking at him I seen he was frustrated so I needed to ease his mind a little. I walked over to the stereo and popped in my R&B Love Zone cd. It had every R&B

Lynaia Jordan

love song you could think of it was a 3-hour long cd. Then I walked over to the bed and crawled my naked body up next to my husband. I began to whisper his name in his ear. I felt the chill bumps come on his arm, so I knew it was turning him on. I wanted to show him my love, so I decided to start by taking off his night pants. I thought he had on underwear, but he didn't. I then took his manhood and began to tease it with my tongue never letting it go all the way in my mouth. Once I felt his head protruding, I decided it was time to take it all in. I went up and down and tongue swirling all over his dick. It was like I was in another world. I felt like the queen of head at this moment, like I had a point to prove and with the way Clyde was moving and grabbing my head I could tell he was understanding my point. I felt the beat in his dick, so I lifted up and kissed his stomach until I was sitting on top of him and I began to ride. Looking him dead in the eyes. I knew he was at his climax because he flipped me over and began to hit it from the back like I was a bad child that needed a spanking. He had to make sure I was satisfied first, and he had no problem at doing it. I was almost at the point of no return when his cell phone rung. He stopped dead in the middle of his tracks and went to get the phone. I turned around with a look on my face like what the fuck.

Clyde began to put on his clothes and then turned to me with "Baby, I have to run I will be right back I promise."

Sun said "What the fuck do you mean you have to run? You better run that chocolate dick up in me!"

Lynaia Jordan

He ignored everything I said and ran out the door into the car and sped off. I jumped up a looked out the window and all I seen was smoke from the car. All he gonna see is smoke coming from my head when he returns!

I paced the floor all night and I knew that something had to be very important for him to leave me like that. I just hope that coming back to Baltimore wasn't a bad idea. I finally decided to lay down and before I knew it, I was sleep.

Chapter Fifteen
Clyde

All I could think is what the fuck is she doing calling me. I don't have shit to say to her at this point. She knows the rules. Damn!!! I pulled up to the Senator theater, walked around the back and there she was sitting in her car. I opened up the passenger door.

"What do you want?"

"Clyde, I had to see you and thank you for everything that you did for me while I was locked up."

"Peaches, didn't I tell you to never call me?"

"I know Clyde but what did you expect to come to Baltimore and not talk to me?"

"Look, you know this is not right. Even back then it wasn't, I have moved on and you should too."

"Clyde I am a changed woman. I don't think that we will be together, you married my enemy even after I told you who she was."

"I know but I fell in love with her. I paid you all the money you asked for. I thought you were over this once you got Mr. Meth back?"

"I thought I was too until I realized that he will always love her and now you are the same way with her. What is it? she has pussy of gold?"

"Naw Peaches it's that she is loyal! A quality you will never have. I can't trust you that's why I came tonight. You may say that you have changed but I still see the same Peaches that hate Sun and will do anything to have her out the picture!"

"For the record, I don't hate the bitch anymore! I just want to tell you that I am thankful for what you did and not to let your guard down around Meth. He loves Sun and he's not gonna stop until he gets her back! This is going to be your real test Clyde and let's see if she is loyal! Now get the fuck out my car before I rape your sexy chocolate ass!"

I got out the car, and as I was walking all I could think about is Peaches haven't changed, Meth loving my wife and me killing him!

I decided that I didn't want to go straight home so I hit the old after hour bar where my boys use to hang. As soon as I walked through the door, I got mad love. James was still in his same spot with the chick Ashley right by his side. Only this time Ashley then got a little older and thicker. James just got older.

"My nigga Clyde. What brings you to this part of the world?"

"What's up James, I'm here on family vacation and I decided to swing past to see who would be in here, I should have known you were here with Ashley."

"Yup Ashley my baby she aint going nowhere, except for going to get us some drinks."

He gave her a look and she got up and said, "Clyde what do you want to drink?"

"I would like a shot of Tang with a glass of sprite soda."

James started to laugh "Nigga you still drinking that same old ass drink. I remember when you and Peaches use to sit and drink that shit. Have you talked to her?"

"Yeah Man, she can't let shit go for real. I'm not the same man from before. I am in love with my wife and she is the one not Peaches."

"My bad Clyde, my bad. I thought that you married Peaches and moved her away because she hasn't been around or you. Then streets aint talking like it use too so I don't know shit. The last thing I heard was you had a kid and was moving out of town then you were gone."

"Yeah, James, I got so caught up in Peaches shit that I just had to leave before shit got hot for me. You know?"

"Yup I can dig it. Well drink up tonight it's on me."

I drank so much that night I ended up sleeping at the bar with James and Ashley. Once I woke up it was seven in the morning. Oh, shit this is not like me I have never stayed out all night. Sun is going to kill me. I jumped in my car and hurried to my mom's house. I opened up the door and everyone was still sleep so I just laid on the couch and acted like I feel out right there.

The smell of pancakes, bacon, scrapple, grits, eggs, sausage and biscuits woke me up. I walked in the kitchen to see my mom's cooking us breakfast.
"Good Morning ma."

"Good Morning Clyde, you want a glass of orange juice or ginger ale?"

"Can I have some ginger ale please ma."

"Well Clyde I don't mean to be in your business but what in the hell do you think you doing, coming in here seven o'clock in the morning?"

Lynaia Jordan

I had a massive headache and I didn't feel like explaining myself to my mother because I know that I would have to explain to Sun, so I just said I was sorry. I went into the guess bathroom washed my face and rinsed out my mouth before I went to talk to Sun. As I was walking back in the kitchen Sun was sitting at the breakfast table pouring her a glass of juice.

"Good Morning Sun."

She kept on doing what she was doing. Pretty much ignoring me.

"Mother I am going to wake the kids after we eat, we are going to go over my mothers for a little while. Did you need me to help you with anything?"

"No baby just goes right ahead."

As Sun walked up the stairs, I grabbed her she turned around and gave me a look that I never seen her look before, so I decided to just let her cool off for a while. I took a shower and by time I got out the shower they were gone.

"Damn she didn't even say goodbye."
    I guess I will go take care of some business and pick up some make up gifts for my wife.

Lynaia Jordan

After taking care of something I headed to the mall to get Sun something special. When I got there, I saw Joy in the jewelry store.

"Hey Joy, what are you doing I her?"

"Nuffin just window shopping, while Sun is there with our mother, I decided to take a break. Shopping always help me out."

"Oh, cause I'm here trying to find ya sister something. You want to help me?"

"Sure, are you looking for jewelry, clothes, purse, shoes?"

"I don't know I was thinking about a necklace. What do you think?"

"I think that you did something really bad to be buying jewelry and it's not her birthday or Christmas."

"Not that bad, but I was wrong."

"Well knowing my sister jewelry won't change anything. Just be honest and she will understand. Flowers and a maybe a bracelet will work!"

Lynaia Jordan

I can't tell Sun the truth but for Joy to be young she was right. Sun is not one of them type of females to hold grudges long. Well except for Peaches!

"Thanks Joy I know just what I'm going to do."

I gave Joy a hug and rushed out the mall. I stopped past the flower shop and then headed back to my mother's house. See no one really knows me. I have done a lot in my past that I'm not proud of but when I saw Sun all of that changed. She made me better. I changed for her. I still dabbled a little, but I honestly changed for her.

When I pulled up to my mother's house, I noticed that Peaches car was in the driveway. What the hell do this bitch think she is doing. I walked in the house to her my mother laughing with Peaches.

"Yes, he was the cuties little boy."

"Hey baby, look who stopped by. I haven't seen her in a long time."

"Hello Peaches, how are you?" I said with a fire look in my eyes.

"Hello Clyde, I have been fine. I actually came to see you. Is it somewhere we could go to talk ion private?"

"Sure, ma will you excuse us for a second?"

"Yes, honey. Peaches it was good seeing you and you need to come around more so you can meet my daughter in law and grandkids."

"That sound great. I will try."

When my mother left out the kitchen, I grabbed that bitch by the arm.

"What the fuck do you think you are doing here, in my mother's house?"
"First of all, you better let my arm go!" She said that looking me straight in my eyes.

"I am here because I needed to tell you something."

"Look come on Peaches and spit it out cause if Sun comes here and see you. It won't be pretty on ya part!"

"Boy please cause if Meth knew I was here he would flip as well. Anyway, I will be brief. I overheard Meth saying he was going to attend the class reunion of Sun's. I didn't work hard and do hard time for you to lose her and me to lose Meth, so you better take care of ya business."

Oh really "Ok, I got this now you get out."

Lynaia Jordan

As Peaches walked away, I forgot about how phat she was. I could hit that again. My mother tapping on my shoulder brought me out of my daze.

"Hey ma what's going on?"

"Look Clyde I remember that girl and she wasn't nice at all, so whatever you have going on with her keep it away from home. Sun is a wonderful woman and she don't deserve that."

My mother just walked away from me. I didn't say a word because I knew she was right and if anyone ever found out how I got with Sun it will be over between us. I have to go to this party with her or at least pick her up from there. I need to work a plan up and I need to do it fast the party is in a couple of days. But first I have to make up for last night!

Lynaia Jordan

Chapter Sixteen
Sun

After I stepped out of the shower, I hurried put my clothes on and headed out. I needed to spend some time with my mother and I really need someone to talk too. Times like this I wish Ruby was here with me. I had to pull over because I felt a break down coming on. I sat there for like twenty minutes crying. I was crying about my mother, crying that I didn't have Ruby, crying because Clyde stayed out all night and think I don't know.

This was one of the reasons why I didn't want to come back to Baltimore. It held only pain for me. I was pain and tears free in Georgia. I need to get myself together. I opened up the overhead mirror so that I could look at my face. When I looked in the mirror, I saw a man walking towards my car. I panicked and hurried and locked the door. He knocked on the window and when I recognized the face, I was relieved.

"Excuse me mame are you ok?"

I opened my car door and stepped out then he really had a chance to see my face.
"Oh my, Sun Jordan. I never thought that I would see your beautiful face again around here."

Lynaia Jordan

"Hey Leon, I am back in town for the reunion. How have you been?"

Leon stood 5 foot 8, about 180-pound, brown skin and bald head, beautiful white teeth, tattoos on his arms. I couldn't see his body because he had on loose fitting pants and shirt.

"Sun I been great, working and trying to keep my mind clear you know."
"Yeah I know! I have been doing the same thing."
I searched is hand to see if he a had a ring on, but he didn't. I remember the last night we were together.

May 23, 1998............. We were at my aunt house baby-sitting while she went to her night job. Leon came over to keep me company, but I knew that was not all that he wanted.

"Sun come on wont me and you go in ya aunt room, the kids are ok they are watching t.v."

"Boy no, if my aunt come in this house while you are here, and we are in her room I am going to be in trouble."

"Man, Sun you are just a tease. You get me all wound up then you drop me off in a bad place."

134

"Well look Leon if you are looking for something more than you need to find a new girl because I am not ready to give up my good stuff yet."

"Sun, maybe I will find a new girlfriend."

That night my feelings were hurt, and I think I had my first heart break. The next day at school he didn't even look my way. He did exactly what he said he found a new girlfriend and she gave it up. Shamere fast ass Benjamin. She gave it up because she knew I didn't and that was ok with him. I never spoke to Leon after that, so it was good seeing him now.

"So, Sun, I don't want to hatch up old memories, but I never got a chance to tell you that I was sorry for how I treated you back in the day. Every time I got the nerve to talk to you, you would walk the other way. Then what happened with Ruby I didn't know how to come to you. I just wanted to let you know that I am truly sorry."

I'm trying to stop the tears from falling out my eye's, so I changed the subject and put my big girl panties on.

"Leon don't even think about that. It was a long time ago. I am a married woman now and I have children it just really good to see that life has been treating you well."

He smiled and yes, I remember his smile.
"Ok, then Sun I will see you Friday!"

Lynaia Jordan

"Ok, Leon I will see you then."

I turned around to get into my car and it felt like someone was still watching me. I looked around and I see nothing but cars and people driving them.

Finally making it to my mother's house, she was up cooking breakfast.

"Hey ma."

"Good Morning, Sun how was your night."

"Ma it was something we need to talk about today. But first you go get dressed because we have some shopping to do."

My mother went upstairs to slip on her clothes and I just walked around down stairs looking at the pictures on the wall like it was my first time in this house. It just seems so unreal when I look at the pictures of me and Ruby. I really miss my best friend I wish she was here with me to laugh and joke and see our children grow up together. I decided that I want to take a drive, so we went to the outlets in VA. My mother was up for it and she looked good too. Maybe I needed to come back to Baltimore to get my mother's health in order.

We made it to the outlets and by the look on my mother's face she was happy we made it. We shopped, we got stuff for the house, her bedroom, my house in GA, the kids, Clyde, and even Joy. We were half way through our day out and I decided that we needed to get something to eat. We chose to eat at Cracker Barrel. Their food is so good.

My mother said "Sun I haven't been here in years. This food is so good."

I just laughed and said I know but this was the time I wanted to talk to my mother.

"So, ma can we talk a little?"

"Sure, whats on ya mind?"

"Well the first thing is I want to say I'm sorry for moving all the way to Georgia and just trying to shut everyone out. Then the next thing is that I need some advice. Ma, I love my husband and he is wonderful, but Ma I have a soft spot in my heart for Meth it's like we were meant to be together. He always completed me."

My mother stopped eating and put her fork down and whipped her mouth then she said "Sun, it was ok that you moved to Georgia you just stayed away so long that was all I missed you and the kids. Then the thing about you heart. Love is a funny thing baby. You can't tell ya heart who to love. You just have to use your mind also. If you are unhappy with Clyde, then it's no reason for you to still be married but if you are happy and yall just going through a little rough spot then make ya marriage work. As for that soft spot in ya heart for Meth. He is and will forever be your first true love baby and so if he has a spot then that's ok. Sun you have to see everything that you have to gain and to lose. Will it all be worth it to lose or gain."

"Ma, I understand, and I know that it going to be ok and me and Clyde is going to be together. Ma, I have something to tell you."

"What your pregnant? No, you sleep with Meth already. No wait goes ahead tell me."

"Ok, so last night Clyde left out in the middle of the night didn't come back until this morning smelling like a bar and then had the nerve to act like he was sleep on the couch all night."

"Wow Sun, so do you think he was with another woman?"

"Ma I never had a thought in my mind about Clyde because he never gave me a reason to doubt him but since we have been back in Baltimore, he has changed a little."

"Baby don't go looking for nothing let it come to you. Everything that is done in the dark come out in the light believe me I am a living witness to that saying. Just keep your eyes open and your ears closed. Excuse me I have to go to the bathroom really quick."

When my mother got up to go to the bathroom, I noticed that I had two missed text messages. One was from Clyde and the other one was from Meth.

Clyde: (Sun I am sorry baby for last night could you meet me at Rocky Point state park @ 7 I have a surprise for you.)

I just smiled cause it typical for a man to try and kiss up after he did something wrong.

Meth: (Hey Sun it's me Meth just wanted you to know that the kids are good, and I will drop them off tonight if they want to come home but if not, they are cool with staying another night with me. Oh, and I had an amazing day yesterday with you and the kids. Just wanted to let you know that my queen)

This man is crazy! I can't do this with Meth I just can't!
As my mother was walking back to the table, I saw the tiredness look in her eye's, so I decided to call it a day. We drove back home, and I knew I didn't want to meet Clyde @7. I wanted him to wait around for me. I knew that he would be blowing up my phone since the kids were with Meth again tonight.

"Ok ma, have a good night."

"You too Sun and Oh baby one thing I forgot to tell you about our little talk earlier. Sun you have to pray and trust that God will guide you the right way."

"Ok Ma" gave my mother a hug and start to head towards when my phone rung and it was an anonyms number.

"Hello, hello well if you are not going to say anything, I am going to hang up, but you have a great night."

I just hung the phone up. Just thinking that it was a wrong number. I gonna stop past the bar tonight because I think that I want a glass of wine. It was a bar on the way to Clyde's mother's house. I stepped in the bar and it was crowded. I hurried and walked to the counter and ask the lady could she tell we the wine is?

"It over there in the cooler with the large grape on it and if you want it warm it's in the back on the second shelf."

"Thank you"

I walked to the back because I knew that it would be a little cheaper and I like ice in my drinks anyway. As I reached for the bottle of wine, I felt like someone was watching me, so I turned really fast, but no one was looking at me and no one looked familiar. I just grabbed the wine and got out of there. I made it to Clyde's mother's house and I really wanted to just relax so I called Clyde.

Lynaia Jordan

"Hey Baby, are you on your way?"

"No Clyde I am not coming I had a long day and I really just want to relax so I am going to just stay in, and I will just see you whenever you decide to come in." Then I hung up the phone in his ear. I laughed in the inside. I want to rest up because I am not going to be stressing and going to this reunion a mess!

Lynaia Jordan

Chapter Seventeen
Peaches

Freedom is what I have and the only thing I have on my mind is getting back at them both. All these years have passed, and I don't feel anything for Meth or Sun. I played my cards wrong then I learned from mistakes and I won't let that happened this time. He thought he was the only one with shit up his sleeve. What I don't understand is why every guy that see this bitch falls in love with her and then either wants to leave me or use me to get to her? This is some fucked up shit but I'm gonna do what I need to, to get back at her ass. I haven't forgotten the day she left for out of town. I owe that bitch something.

"Hey Keith baby are you off, yet I want to stop pass to see you?"

"No Peaches I'm not off. I will meet you at my house in like 2 hours. Is that cool?"

"Yup that's great. Are you ok you just sound a little weird?"

"Yeah baby everything is fine."

"Ok, just checking I will be there in two hours."

Lynaia Jordan

When I hung up the phone with him. I already knew what the problem was the same problem all these niggas have Sun! OOOHH I can't stand that bitch! I can't go to Meth house because he doesn't know if Sun can take seeing me yet! I have to wait to be with Keith because he still hooked on her! Then Clyde, he got her and don't even know that he gonna have to fight to keep her! I go over there to give him a warning and he don't even listen he all caught up with her. You know what (shaking her head) ummmm Clyde is the key and I am getting ready to be in attack mode. (rubbing her hands together) tomorrow my plan will begin!

I drove over to Keith's house and he was sitting there waiting for me so we could go in together.

He said "Hey Peaches "as he gave me a kiss.

"Hey Keith, you had a hard day of work?" I asked as we were going into the door.

"Naw, just the same old, same old. A lot of paperwork today. I am working on a new case. This one is big."

"It doesn't anything to do with me again do it? My hands are clean." I asked in a joking manner.

"Girl No, matter of fact it has no connection to you at all. We are past all of that. I want to build with you

Peaches. We have been going strong for three years and it's not a secret that you have done wrong but the new you have made me fall in love with you."

Before I knew it, Keith was down on one knee asking me to marry him. Oh, my goodness!!

"Yes, Keith I will marry you, but wait Keith you were the one that wanted to keep us a secret for the past three years because you didn't know how people would take it. Keith you may lose your job over this. Wait I don't want that to happen. I can't except your proposal. I won't let you do that to yourself. Not for me. We can still be together. It will work out. Now get up."

"See Peach this is why I love you. Baby you are the best. I do want you and Earl to move in with me. Can we work on me meeting him and see if he would be ok with moving in here with me?"

"Baby I will talk to him, but I will not promise you anything. Let's eat some dinner and go to bed cause I'm tired too."

After we ate, I needed to get some rest. I'm a bitch but I couldn't get married to a cop and I know the things that I be involved in."

Lynaia Jordan

The next morning Keith was already gone but this morning he left a key on the nightstand. I grabbed it and put it on my hook. Today was going to be a crazy one but I needed to get it started so I could make my move.

I went to see Melik and Earl but to my surprise Sun's daughter and Son was at the house. Meth didn't tell me they were staying the night.

I walked in the house and everyone was sitting at the breakfast table like a happy family. Meth had a dick look on his face when I walked in the kitchen.

"Well good morning everyone. I see no one called me for breakfast?"

"Good Morning Peaches." Meth said No one called you because you weren't invited."

When he said that Sun's son had a smirk on his face.

"Well I just invited myself." I walked over to give Melik and Earl a kiss and a hug.

"So, I see you have company and by the looks on their face they must be your twins?"

"Yes, Peaches this is Meth we call him Junior and this is Meshun we call her Mee-Mee."

145

Lynaia Jordan

The little girl smiled but the little boy just mugged me.

"Hello, I'm Peaches Melik and Earl's mother. It's nice to finally me you."

"Hello Ms. Peaches. It is nice to finally see you." Mee-Mee said.

Junior didn't say anything he just got up from the table and walked towards the steps in the hallway. Meth hurried up and ran behind him. I know that I need to hurry up and leave because this little girl looks just like her mother and I can't take looking in her face this morning.

"Earl, I need to talk to you about something later when you get some time and Melik I will be back tomorrow. I want to go see that movie you wanted to see. I think it's Batman Begins."

"Yup that's it. Well that's cool can my brother and sister come with us?"

"Well I don't think that their mother would like that but if you want to wait that will be ok also."

"yeah I think I want to wait. I'm having a good time with them."

Mee-Mee smiled and said "See you later Ms. Peaches"

146

Lynaia Jordan

" See you later sweetie." I said but I didn't mean it and I know that its mean, but she looks just like my enemy!

I decided to call Clyde to see if he can meet me tomorrow night at the bar. I wanted to see him.

(Hey, you know who this is can you meet me at the bar tomorrow before you pick up your wife from her reunion?")

I waited a minute because I know this nigga don't want me to a call his phone.

Ding (ok, and stop texting me early in the morning with your crazy ass)

I just laughed because he is a chicken shit and I know it. He is weak and I can believe that I ever fucked with a weak nigga like him!

I went and ate breakfast got me a new outfit for tomorrow and then I headed to the car wash. I wanted to talk to Meth and Earl. I think it's time that Meth knows the truth about me and Keith. You know I really don't care what he thinks I just want him to know.

When I pulled up at the car wash it was jumping! Meth was making that cash and all he had to do was snap a finger and he would have women falling at his feet. Wait there is Sun's son sitting in the car but where is the other

Lynaia Jordan

kids. I stepped in the car wash and started to walk over to his office when I heard Meth yelling to someone. So, I stood by the door and listened.

"Meth I don't give a fuck about her all I care about is our children. See this is why I didn't want to come back here cause of shit like this."

"Sun listen I can explain. I tried everything in my power to keep Peaches away from the kids but what do you want me to do. Stop my fucking son to not see his mother because you and she had a beef 10, 15 years ago. Sun that is crazy. You need to let this shit go she has changed. She cannot come between anything anymore."

"Right Meth, she can come between anything cause its nothing there, but this bitch tried to take everything away from me because of you! I will be to get Mee-Mee this evening and they will no longer stay the night at you house."

"Ok Sun, I don't want to fight with you I love you and the kids with all my heart."

As he was saying that I could hear him getting closer to the door, so I decided to act like I was ready to knock on the door.

Knock, Knock

Lynaia Jordan

"Didn't I tell you I was bus" that nigga stop in his tracks when he saw my face then he turned to look at Sun.

That bitch hasn't changed one bit and she knew it. But I greeted her with a smile. She walked pass me with her head up high. I had to say something to her I just had to.

"Meth did I interrupt something?"

"No Peaches what's up?"

"I will be right back I need to tell Sun something."

He yelled after me not to, but I ignored him.

"Sun, excuse me Sun"

This pretty bitch better not crack slick cause I'm going to bust her ass if she does. She stopped and turned to me.

"Sun, I wanted to tell you that I was sorry for all the pain I caused you and I hope that you can forgive me."

She stepped close to me and I was ready for her too this time.

"Peaches listen to me and I hope you hear me well. I will never forgive you and I hope that you don't ever approach me again, because if you do, I might have a flash back and whip that ass!!"

Sun turned and got in her car. Meth was running over to us from the door of the car wash. Oh, ok, I got this bitch she thinks I took Meth from her. She really gonna go crazy when she finds out her husband was mine first!

"Meth I only was trying to tell her that I was sorry for everything that happened, and she came incorrect, but I let it slide."

"I know Peaches she is still in her feelings but what are you doing here?"

"Well I came pass this morning to talk to you about something we couldn't talk so I decided to come pass and talk to you. Do you have time right now to talk?"

"Yeah come on in my office."

When we walked in the office, I had a seat at his desk and crossed my legs.

"Ok, what's up Peaches?"

"Ard so I have something to tell you. You might be mad at me, but I am happy and that's all that matters."

Lynaia Jordan

"What is it girl as long as Melik and Earl is ok I'm good."

"Ok, so you remember the detective Keith?"

"Yeah I remember his ass."

You can see the wrinkles forming in Meth forehead he is getting angry.
"Well for the past three years I have been seeing him and he asked me to marry him last night I told him no, but I am going to move in with him, me and Earl."

Meth jumped up and paced the floor then he turned to me and said

"WHAT THE FUCK IS YOUR DUMB ASS THINKING. HE IS A FUCKING COP MATTER OF FACT THE COP THAT PUT YOU AWAY! Yo I can't be happy for you, I can't tell you what to do but my son aint coming over and We gonna have to stay away from each other. Man, yall bitches just can't let go of shit. You just doing this shit to get back at Sun! Man, you aint change Peaches you still the same ole sneaky ass bitch from before! Get the fuck out of my office I can't take you right now!"

I just got up and walked out. He really gonna be pissed at me when he sees what's coming next.

Lynaia Jordan

Chapter Eighteen
Peaches

"Keith, I told Meth he was upset but, I don't care. Me and Earl are moving in with you."

"This is wonderful baby, let's take the boys out to meet each other officially and eat dinner."

"That sound good. Keith what about work?"

"Peaches, let me worry about that."

"Ok, but have to change my address and everything, so are you sure this is what you want?"

"Baby, I have never wanted anything more. I love you and you make me happy."

I jumped on him and kissed him all over.

"Keith let me go freshen up."

I picked up my phone and called the boys first.

"Earl, tell your brother to get something on we are going out for dinner in an hour. I know his other peoples are there, but they can't come."

"Ard Ma I will let him know."

152

Lynaia Jordan

After I hung up with the boys, I texted Clyde and let him know we needed to talk. He hasn't responded back to me, but I know he will. You know what I'm ready to call him.

"Hello"

Did this he just hang-up on me. I know he didn't, I called the line back.

"Hey Clyde, you better not hang up!"

"What Peaches, didn't I tell you don't just call my phone, I seen ya text damn."
"Look we need to talk."

"What, ok, so what do we need to talk about?"

"Well this is something I can't say over the phone."
"Ard, so when?"

"The night of the reunion, Keith and Sun will be there, so we don't have to make no excuses."

"Ard, once I drop her off, I will meet you at the bar."

"Ard, don't be late either."

"Bye, Peaches and stop calling my fucking phone."

When we arrived at the restaurant Keith was already there, he orders our drinks and appetizers.

"Keith, this is my son Earl and my son Melik."
" Hey boys, nice to meet you."
Earl spoke but Melik didn't.
"Melik, what is your problem? Now Mr. Keith said hello"

"Hello, Mr. Keith."

"Hey Melik."

"Peaches, come on and sit down."

"So, Boys, I wanted us to have dinner together because Mr. Keith asked me a very important question, well two of them."

Melik face was so red and he aint even light skin.
"So, ma, you gonna marry the man that put you in jail?"

"Melik, he didn't put me in jail, I put myself there by the crazy decisions I made."

"Go head ma, Melik will be ok."

"Thank you, Earl, so he asked me to marry him and for me and Keith to move in with him. I am not making any decision unless you two are ok with it. You two are my world."

"Well ma, it's cool with me he seems like a decent dude, and it's your life. I really don't know about Melik."

"Melik baby, do you give me your blessing?"

"No, I do not, he took you away from me, and it's not right I will never forgive him. If he loved you, he would have helped you be home, so that you could take care of your son. I am calling my father right now to come and get me and yall three can have a family dinner because I will never be a part of this."

Melik left the table, I didn't run after him he truly don't know who his mother is.

"Keith, I'm sorry baby, it's going to be ok. He will come around."

Lynaia Jordan

Chapter Nineteen
Sun

"How do I look?"

It was night of my reunion party. For the past two days me and Clyde or Meth haven't spoken to each other. I guess Clyde is mad because I wouldn't except his apology yet. Then Meth mad cause I won't let Junior come back over with him.

"Really" Junior said, he didn't want to go back over there himself.

My mother, Mee-Mee, Junior, and Joy was sitting there while I was getting dressed.

"Ma you look beautiful" said Junior

"Yes, baby you look like you did 10 years ago. I'm so glad that I was here to see you go." Said my mother

"Yeah ma Junior is right you look beautiful. I can't wait until I go to my prom because I know I'm gonna look beautiful too!" Mee-Mee said smiling.

156

Lynaia Jordan

I looked at Joy waiting for her to say something, but she didn't she just looked and smiled. Since we have been back in Baltimore Joy has been treating me so different. Tomorrow I want to do a sister date with her but for now the smile will do.

I was ready I walked out to the car and the whole block was out like I was ready to go to prom for real. I had on a white fitting dress that had a choker neck strap and sheer down the middle of the front the showed a little of my inner breast. Clear stilettoes, jewelry and a little clutch. My hair was pinned up in a messy bun with a few pieces of hair dangling from the back and front. I did look good and from the look on my husband face he was pleased. Clyde opened the door up for me and told the kids he would be right back to take them to his mother's house.

Junior said, "Dad we gonna stay with grandma tonight yall have fun."

Clyde said ok and then we pulled off at first it was silence in the car, then Clyde said, "Sun can we talk?"

I looked at him because I really didn't have anything to say but I answered him.

"Yes, Clyde we can talk."

I turned my body to face him while he was driving. He pulled over.

Lynaia Jordan

"First baby I want to tell you that you look beautiful. Then I want to say I'm sorry for the other night. I had to take care of some business and then I stopped at a bar and I got drunk before I knew it, it was morning. Baby I'm sorry I would never hurt you baby."

"Clyde thank you and I accept your apology. Once you pick me up from the reunion we can talk."

"ok baby that's fine."

When we pulled up to the reunion, I was nervous. I knew that I would have to face a little more of my past and I didn't know how I would take it. Clyde grabbed my hand then said, "Have fun tonight, and I will be here when you call." He gave me a kiss and I got out the car.

I walked into the building and headed towards the music. I immediately saw Sangela and Sashley. They were the organizers for our class.

"Omg, is that Sun Jordan."

"Girl Sun you haven't changed a bit, did she Kashley?" Kangela said

"Hey twins. I see yall still looking youthful. So, what are yall doing now?"

Lynaia Jordan

"Well Kangela and I own our own clothing boutique called the Logan Sisters on 23rd and Holmes Lane. You should come pass we have some cute stuff." Kashley said.

"Ok I will before I head back out of town."

"Girl it's thick in there. People brought tickets that wasn't even in our graduating class but went to the school before us or after us. Have fun here's you raffle ticket and don't forget to cast your vote for class reunion King and Queen."

"Ok, ladies I will see you inside."

When I walked through the doors, she wasn't lying it was thick in here. I just wanted to find a seat see my girls and go home. The music was jumping, and the food smelled so good. I looked across the room and there was my cousin Ray, my home girl Hedah and Oh no they weren't standing the with Shamere. I walked over to them and Ray saw me coming and she immediately ran to me.

"Sun" she yelled

"Hey Ray, I miss you. We haven't talked since you came back to Baltimore."

"I know girl I have been so busy. Me and Trey got engaged last week. Right about time."

Lynaia Jordan

"Yes, Ray that is beautiful Mee-Mee gonna be so happy."

"Hedah"
"Hey Sun girl it's been a long time, but ya pretty tail still looked the same."

Just then I felt someone come up behind me and put their hands over my eyes. I could hear Ray sucking her teeth.

"Excuse me who is this?" I said
The male voice said, "Take a guess."
"No, I'm not guessing just take your hands off my eyes and I will be able to see who it is." I was agitated cause my makeup was gonna be messed up. When I turned around it was Keith.

"Keith, hey, how are you?"

"Sun hey that's all I get no hug or anything."

"I'm sorry Keith" I gave him a slight hug

Does he really think that I would be excited to see him? He is crazy. I turned my attention back to Ray and

Lynaia Jordan

Hedah. By this time Shamere was gone. So, I'm kind of glad Keith came over to speak.

"Come on yall lets go dance like we use to take over the whole school dance."
"Sun we are too old to be dancing like that I got bad knees." Said Hedah

We all just busted out laughing because she said that. I headed to the floor and the DJ was jamming. I totally forgot about Keith, Clyde and Meth. My phone rung and it was Clyde, aww so sweet he was thinking about his baby.

"Hey Baby."
The phone hung up and when I tried to call back, it went straight to voicemail. He must don't have no service. I was dancing so much that I need a drink, but I didn't want to go over their cause Leon was getting a drink and I didn't want anyone to get any ideas. You know what freak what they think I looked up at the slide show that was playing the whole night and saw Me and Ray at a basketball game. Then me and Hedah in the State math competition. They had pictures of everything.
Then I see it the picture that would mess my whole night up. Me and Ruby on year book picture the best friends! It stopped me in my tracks, and I ran off the dance floor. I don't know where all the tears came from, but they were there, and I couldn't stop them. Hedah and Ray ran after me.
"Sun waits!" Ray said

Lynaia Jordan

"Girl are you ok?" asked Hedah.

    I stopped and turned to the "I'm fine yall I just wasn't ready for that. You know? I'm gonna call Clyde so he could come get me. I want to go home and relax."
    Leon must have seen me run out of the room.
    "Sun are you ok?"
    "Yeah Leon, I'm ok, it just took me back a little you know."
    "Yup, I know, just like the first time I seen you after all these years."
    It was a little quite so Ray shouted.
    "Ard Cuz, give me love."
    I snapped out of it.
    "Ard Ray and Hedah Love yall, Ray I'm gonna call you cause we got to plan a wedding." I said with a partial smile. Leon thanks for making sure I was ok."
    "No problem Sun have a good night."
    I keep trying to call Clyde and he didn't answer his phone it must be dead because it is going straight to voicemail.
    "What the hell!"

    I'm gonna just call Joy. Damn her shit is going straight to voicemail too. I'm just gonna have to call Meth.
    "Whats up Sun"

Lynaia Jordan

"Meth I need a ride home. Clyde is not answering, and Joy isn't either. Do you think that you can come pick me up please?"

"Ok, I will be there in 15 minutes. I walked out the building and waited for him outside. I didn't want anyone to see him pick me up. I tried calling Clyde several more times and no answer. I need to know what is going on. Meth pulled up in 15 minutes like he said he would. I opened the car door and sat down.

Standing outside I felt like someone was watching me, but I didn't see anyone. I wish Meth hurry up.

"Thank you, Meth, I'm not sure why Clyde didn't answer, but thank you."

"Sun, whats wrong?"
"Nothing I'm ok Meth"
"Why are you crying?"

I couldn't hold it in any longer, "they put a picture up of me and Ruby, Meth I miss her so much. She was my best friend, the only person that understood me. It's like she turned her back on me. Why Meth Why?"

He pulled the car over and turned to me.

"Sun, if no one in this world knows how you feel it's me. I lost my brother, my ace, my right-hand man. He was the selfish one. Nothing was never enough for him. He had to have it all, he couldn't just be her boyfriend, he had to marry her. I am so sorry Sun for everything I brought to your life all the pain, hurt, heartache, everything Sun."

"Meth there you go making it about me and you. Ruby didn't die because of you and me it was because, she couldn't live knowing that she wasn't the one for her husband."

"Sun, no, it's me. He didn't want to talk to her, it was only because, I wanted you. He knew it."

"Meth they were selfish, I just needed to get this off my chest, it hurt me to see that picture."

"Sun, do you have to go home?"

"No, why?"

"I want to chill, is that ok, no strings attached, just two friends, taking a drink and reminiscing."

"Let me see if Clyde is ok first."

I tried calling Clyde again and no answer, ok he is doing him.

"Meth, let's go"

"Ok, before we head there, I have to shoot over West to pick up this money."

Lynaia Jordan

"Meth, I'm not for that tonight."

"No." he laughed "This is for Melik, his classmate dad owes me some money for the trip to the beach for his son. He works over west as a bartender at night."

"Oh, because you know!"
"I know Sun, I wouldn't do that to you."
We pulled up over west and the bar was like a little hole in the wall. Wait I know that's not Clyde's car. Naw it couldn't be.

"You know what, I don't like the surroundings, I am just gonna get it from him tomorrow."

Meth pulled off so fast, it looks like he seen Clyde's car too.

He drove to Cocky Lou's, picked up a fifth of Henny and a two-liter coke soda, some chips and Swedish fish. Then he went to the park. Parked the car and told me to get out. Ok Sun keep it together, it aint the 90's and yall not together.

"Sun you not getting out the car. Oh, I know what is missing."
He went into the trunk pulled out a box of tapes and cd's.
I opened the car door and stepped out.

Lynaia Jordan

"Meth I know that's not my box of music from college?"

"Sun, wait I'm just gonna let the music do the talking for me."

Music starts to play "ohhhh, baby, oooooooo. You mean the world ooh, and everything that I offer........."

"Come on Sun dance with me?"

So, I stood in the moon light, in my beautiful dress, allowed Meth to grab my hand and we danced like we were the only two on earth. It seemed like the song played forever. He played my whole cd. We drank, danced, sat on top of the car, laughed, cried. It was like Meth wanted to say something, but he didn't, we just enjoyed the moment. He looked at his watch.

"Wow its late, come on Sun, let me get you home."

We got in the car and drove to my mother's house. No words were said. I got out the car and opened the door. I didn't even look back, he just pulled off.

Chapter Twenty
Clyde

Wow, my wife looked so beautiful, "Lord please forgive me."

I headed over to the bar because I know if I didn't show she would act crazy. When I walked in the bar, she wasn't there yet so I order a beer.

"Hey Clyde, come over here with us. twice in a week, whats up man?"

"Yeah man, Peaches is on her way she needed to talk."

"Just like old times huh."

"Hell no, this is not a reunion."

I got time Sun is probably having a great time. I just have to let Peaches know that it's time for her to move on and leave us alone. If she not trying to hear it, then I think that I need to tell Sun the truth.

"Hey, let me get a gin and tonic"

This chick is taking her time, I should call Sun. just to check on her. When I looked up, she was walking through the door. I hurried up and hung the phone up. I turned it off just until I leave here.

"Hey Peaches, whats up"

Lynaia Jordan

"Nuffin much you look nice."

"So, do you, would you like a drink?"

"Yes, my usual, why you not over there with them?"

"I wanted to wait at the bar for you."

"Ok, so I ran into Sun at the Car Wash, she wasn't too happy to see me."

"Did she say anything to you."

"Oh yeah ya little Bitch told me to walk light because she just might have a flash back."

I stated to laugh a little cause the little bitch was funny.

"Peaches, please leave my wife alone. Is that what you wanted to tell me?"

"No, I wanted to tell you to watch out for Meth. He loves Sun and I think she still loves him."

"You don't know what you are talking about., Hey could I get another and make it a double shot."

"Oh, did I push a button?"

"No, I just want another drink. I'm gonna have to leave to go get Sun."

I leaned in close in his face.

"Ok well, I need a ride home could you drop me off?"

"Ok, let me drink this and then we could leave."

His one more drink turned into four, we were tripping tho, I really miss chilling with someone that is cool as shit. Oh, but I know I got him now.

"Clyde you ready?"

"Yeah, Peach baby, I got to let you drive, go to my mother's house so I can call my wife."

"Ok baby."

Lynaia Jordan

"Peaches, I'm not playing with ya little fat fat ass."

"I know Clyde."

I drove straight to the Marriott and let the games begin.

Lynaia Jordan

Chapter Twenty- One
Meth

I know I just didn't see this nigga at the bar. When the fuck he starts hanging out at this bar. I know that this is a hangout of Peaches, I remember that bitch telling me before. Yo I gotta get to the bottom of this.

"Hello, Peaches, this Meth I know that it is late but give me a call once you get this message, I need to talk to you."

Something not right. I woke up the next morning and Peaches aint call me back yet. I'm gonna take the kids out to breakfast, then I'm going to try and call her.

"Melik, do you want to come and eat breakfast with me? We need to talk about the other night."
"Ard dad, I will be ready in 15 minutes."

Let me call Sun to make sure she doesn't have a hangover.

"Good Morning."
"Good Morning, Meth"
"You still in bed?"

"Yeah, I don't feel too well, for some reason my head and stomach hurt."

Lynaia Jordan

"I'm sorry we had a good time last night."

"Yeah we did, thank you for being there when I really needed you.:"

"Well I'm gonna let you sleep, I will come and get the kids if I can later today."

"You can get them, they can defend their self from Peaches, but if she ever hurt my kids she dead!"

"Sun, don't even think like that."

If my suspensions are correct me and you will be together, and she will be out the picture any way.

Me and Melik road to the Ihop on Loch Raven to get something to eat. The service is shitty as fuck.

"So, Melik, what happened at dinner with your mother? I know that night you didn't want to talk about it."
"Well she gonna ask me to give her my blessings to mess with Keith. Daddy, I can't, he took her away from me."

"I understand son, but you didn't disrespect your mother, did you?"

"No, I didn't, I just got up and called you to come get me. But last night, you were singing in your sleep and kept talking to Ms. Sun."

Melik started to laugh

"What!"
"Yeah I heard you come in and it was quite for a minute then I heard singing, I walked over to you and you were sleep singing, saying yeah Sun told you."
"Wow, and you aint even wake me up?"

"Naw that was funny!"

"Whatever! It aint no secret son, I love Ms. Sun. I always have. I one day may have a chance but right now I'm ok with the relationship we have."

"I'm glad you said that. I need to tell you one more thing."

"What is it."

"You gotta promise me you won't say anything but just keep an eye out. Please dad."

"I promise."

"Remember you told me all a man had in this world is his word."

Lynaia Jordan

"Yeah son, I promise."

"Ok, so Meshun like Earl and I think that he likes her too, but he has too much respect for you to talk to her."

Oh, my pressure just went through the roof all I could see was murder.

"So, you mean to tell me your big Sister and Big Brother like each other? Oh, I am keeping an eye out. Thanks for telling me son. I needed to know that."
"I told her that was nasty and no I wasn't hooking them up, but she not listening to me."

"Ok, it's cool, she got her father in her, Huh! I got this. Let's finish eating, I'm gonna stop pass the Car Wash then pick up the twins."

Lynaia Jordan

Chapter Twenty - Two
Mee-Mee

"Hey Connie, what are you doing?"

"Girl nuffin trying on these shorts my mother brought me that I think is too big."

"Send me a picture of them."

"Oh yeah they too small!"

"Ok, so what's been going on with you and your family and how is Junior doing he don't call me or anything. He must have met a little girl up there."

"Naw Connie, he just been chilling with our brother and our God brother that's all. They be playing ball going to the car wash and everything. I be the one that be bored. Trying to stay up under Earl."

I laughed and Connie said "Well ya boy is down here missing you. So have fun this summer because you know what's up there aint gonna last what down here is what's real."

"Yeah, I know you right, but you never know. I am going to call you back later"

Lynaia Jordan

"Ard tell ya brother I said call me."

"Ok"

Once I hung the phone up with Connie I wanted to go over and chill with Earl. Since Meth was trying to spend some time with us. This was the perfect chance to get over there. I walked into my grandmother's kitchen.

"Grandma can I call Meth so that I could see if I could go over his house for a little while?"

"Mee you have to call your mother first and see what she says."

"Ok" so I called my mother and asked her she said it was ok.

"Hello"

"Hey Mee-Mee what going on. Are you ok?"

"Yes, I'm fine. I wanted to know if I could come over your house for a while?"

"Well I'm going to take care of some business so you can come over later on."

I got real quite then he said, "you know what yes, you can come I will be there in 15 minutes to pick you up ok."

"Ok I will be ready I am at grandma's"

"Ok"

I ran back in the kitchen told grandma and then I ran upstairs to freshen up. Meth was there right when he said he would be. When I got into the car, he told me that I would be in the house for like three hours by myself because he had plans already.

"That's cool, I just was tired of sitting in there with my grandmother. My mother is running around taking care of business for my grandmother."

It was just me and him in the car and I was excited to just have a little alone time with my father.

"Hey Meth"

"Mee-Mee you can call me dad or daddy or father something like that."

"I know it just feels weird since I have been calling Clyde that all my life."

I should have not said that, but it was the truth and he need to hear that if he wants to build a father daughter relationship with me.

"I know sweetie I just hope that it could change one day. I'm sorry for not coming after yall and making the right decisions so that we could be together as a family. It was so complicated, and I was young and the only thing I was tired of was hurting your mother, she means so much to me and I just wanted to see her happy that even meant if I had to stay away. I'm sorry Mee-Mee."

"It's cool Meth let's just look forward to the future."

"So, I have to drop you off at the house for like three hours, I already had a meeting set up so is that cool?"

"Yeah, where is Melik and Junior?"

"I dropped them off this morning at the car wash. They did a little job for me. Earl might be in the house but if he not you should be good. I made market, cable games and if it's something you want just call me and I will be right there."

"That's cool. I will find something to do. When you come back could we go see a movie or something?"

"Yup just me and you! It's a date."

Lynaia Jordan

When we pulled up to his house no one was there like he said so I just made something to eat and turned on a good movie. I must have felt asleep I felt someone over me and when I opened my eyes it was Earl. I jumped like I was scared.

"Boy why in the hell are you standing over me?"

"I just got here girl, but I was looking at you. You know you look just like your mother?"

I stretched and then I stood up in his face.

"I guess that was a compliment so thank you."

I was so close that I could have kissed him. His lips looked so good. His breath smelled like a piece of double mint gum. I took two steps back then he said

"Look Mee, I can't go there with you. Like I said I have mad respect for your father. Then you are a little girl to me."

"Earl I'm not a little girl but I will respect your wishes right after I kiss you for the first and last time."

I walked over to him and gave him a kiss at first, he wasn't kissing me back but then he did and then pushed me away. I didn't care because I know that he liked me. I will

178

wait for him to come around I just hope it don't take him all summer.

By time Meth came back to the house Earl left.

"Mee get ya shoes on we are going out!"

So, him and I spent the rest of the day shopping and eating. He dropped me off at Clyde's mother house and said he would call me in the morning because Junior was staying the night with him and the boys.

Chapter Twenty-Three
Clyde

"Fuck, Fuck, Fuck! Where are my pants, what did I do?"

"Clyde its ok, we didn't do anything, I slept on the couch. You were to drink so I drove you to my room and we came here, and you passed out."

"Peaches, are you sure?"

"I said we didn't do anything, now if you want to believe I gave you some of this good shit than, that's on you but I'm not claiming it. First off ya dick wouldn't get hard!"

"Wait, What!"

"Yeah, I tried, but it wouldn't so I left you alone."

"Where is my phone, I left that in your car."

"Ard, Peaches, I am going to be in the fucking dog house."

"I don't give a fuck, fuck he and your house. Get out my hotel room."

Lynaia Jordan

"You crazy, I will call you later."

"Don't call me Clyde."

I walked to my car I felt so bad; I swear I can't drink no more.
"Good Morning Sun"

"Good Morning Baby, I'm sorry, I stayed at my mother's house last night, I was drinking."

"Oh, baby that is ok, I figured that when you didn't call me."

"Clyde, I did call you and you call me back, but I guess your phone went dead. I had a little break down last night. Meth came and picked me up tho."

"What?"

"Clyde, I needed someone to pick me up, you didn't answer. What was I supposed to do, stand outside in a dress like I'm a hooker?"

"No, baby, I'm sorry for tripping. I trust you even though I don't trust him."

"Whatever Clyde what time you gonna come and pick me up?"

Lynaia Jordan

"I'm gonna go take a shower from my morning run and then I will be over there."

"Ok, I should be ready by then."

Yo this was a bad idea, us coming back to Baltimore. Only thing gonna come from this is trouble. I can feel it."

Lynaia Jordan

Chapter Twenty-Four
Sun

"Junior, come help me with this bag."

"Ma, what do you have in this bag?"

"It's a surprise for grandma, you know her birthday is this weekend, I'm gonna throw her a party."

"Ma that is cool, I'm glad that we came up here, I am really having a good time."

"I know, I been having fun too. I miss spending time with my mother."

"I know, it feels right. I'm glad we get to spend our birthday here."

"Yeah me too. I'm so glad that we are all together. Let me call Clyde to see where he is."

As I was standing out there, I have that funny feeling again like someone is watching me, I looked up and down the street and I didn't see no one. I don't know what this feeling is, but I want it to stop.

Lynaia Jordan

"Clyde, where are you?"

"Sun, I am on my way, I'm running a little behind."

"Ok, Clyde, please hurry, I need your help."

"Baby, I'm on my way."

"Oh, Meth is coming too, the kids invited him."
"Sun that is cool."

"Ard, baby I will be waiting."

I hope his occupied time don't have anything to do with that bar. Let me change my mind, I can't think like this.

My mother's party was so much fun, and everyone got along, me Meth and Clyde.

"I would like to thank everyone for coming out to my mother's birthday party. This year has been a rough one, but she made it through to see another one. I love my mother and my sister. My sister took care of my mother when I was here. So, I know this is my mother's party, but I have a special gift for you Joy."
We all walked outside, and I got her a new Acura Coop.

184

Lynaia Jordan

"I love you Joy."

"Sun thank you."

"You are welcomed"

"Come on ma, come dance for us."
My mother got up and started to dance and then she went down on the floor.

"Clyde, Help. Get my mother."

We all ran, and Clyde lifted her up, I called 911, the ambulance came right out. I was a wreck; this is the worst night ever."

We all rushed to the hospital, my mother had to stay there because her sugar was low, she said she didn't want to ruin her appetite earlier, so she just waited to eat.
"Ma, you can't do that."
"I know Sun, it will be ok. I feel better already."
"Ma, it's not ok, you have to take care of yourself."

"Sun, ok, I promise I will do better."

"You better, we don't want to be scare like this again. I'm getting ready to take the kids home. Joy are you gonna."

Before I could finish the sentence, she cut me off.

Lynaia Jordan

"Yeah Sun, I'm not leaving mommies side."

"Thanks Sis, I love you."

My mother kissed the kids and we left."

Lynaia Jordan

Chapter Twenty - Five
Peaches

"Keith come on."

"Peaches, just hold up, we are not going to be late."
"Yes, we are, this is his championship game."

"You know what you and Melik go because he doesn't want me there anyway."
"Look Keith, it has to come to this, either we gonna be together and show the world or I'm gonna move back to my place and call it quits!"

"Peaches don't talk like that."
"Ok so come on."

"Ard let me go get my wallet and stuff and I will be right back down."

Damn, I forgot my damn phone, I need that. As I was walking pass the bathroom, I heard Keith on the phone.

"Look she don't suspect a thing. One of them gonna slip."

Lynaia Jordan

Oh, my fucking goodness, this slick ass nigga trying to set us back up. Oh, I got his bitch ass. I got him. I got my phone and hurried back downstairs.

"Keith come on we are ready."

"Peaches, here I come. Calm down baby."

"Look don't tell me to calm down, my son might not mean shit to you, but he means everything to me. You know what, I just want you to stay here. Come on Earl lets go."

"Ma, you sure."

"Yeah, we already gonna be late."

"Ard, see you later Mr. Keith."

As I was walking to the car, I felt hurt, the real kind. While I was riding, I needed to talk to my son he was all I had, and I had to make him understand that and all so make him my best friend and will have my back no matter what.

"Earl, I have to tell you something, but you can't tell no one."

"Ok Ma."

Lynaia Jordan

"So, Mr. Keith is trying to put me and Meth back in jail. I overheard him on the phone, telling someone, I don't suspect anything and he gonna get all of us this time."

"Ma are you serious."

"Yes baby, but your mother knows now, so I can deal with him accordingly, but I don't have anyone that genuinely have my back."

"Ma, I got your back, I will not allow no one to hurt you. Tell me what we need to do."

"Right now, son, we chill, only move when I tell you to. The other thing is Mr. Clyde was my boyfriend after I met your father. He didn't tell no one."

"Ma, that's crazy!"

"Me and you are the only two that knows this, and I would like to keep it that way."

"Ma, your, secret is safe with me."

"Thank you, baby, I love you so much!"

"I know ma, I love you too."

I have to move fast now, before everything is ruined by Keith.

Lynaia Jordan

Chapter Twenty - Six
Meth

Stuff been so busy, haven't had time to talk about me calling her that night of the reunion. Juggling two families is hard work for real.

"Peaches, He did a great job didn't he?"
"Yeah Meth, you have been doing an awesome job with our son, both of them actually, Earl looks up to you."

"Thanks Peaches, I'm glad you changed, I never thought I would be saying this to you but thank you for being supportive to our son and my situation. So why ya boy Keith didn't come?"

"See you gotta make a good moment go wrong. He had to work and for real Melik don't like him and I didn't want to ruin his night."

"Wow, you really have grown."
"I try."
"Oh, a Peaches you know the boy that's in Melik's class name Shawny?"
"Yeah, why something happened?"
"Naw, Naw, it's just that his father owes me some money and I wanted to know if you could pick it up for me."

Lynaia Jordan

"Yeah sure, you know money talks and bullshit walks."

I laughed a little cause I couldn't wait to see her face reaction when I say where.

"So, you gotta go to that little bar over West, you know the one you use to go to back in the day. Yeah because he asked me meet him there the night of Sun reunion but I had to pick her up so I couldn't go."
Man, Peaches face turned white and right there I knew she had something going on with Clyde.

"Oh yeah, I know which one you are talking about. I could get it. So, you picked up Sun one night and her husband didn't have anything to say about it."
Oh, her snake ass wanna fish, so here we go.

"Well since you wanna know she said she was calling him, and he didn't answer. You know how nigga's is?"
"Yup, I sure do. Meth I'm gonna pick ya money up, so just call me with the time."

"I'm gonna call you with the time in a few minutes."

As she is walking away I can she her back moving like she was laughing. I gotta tell Sun about my suspicions. I don't care if she doesn't believe me or not. Oh, I'm gonna get my family back one way or another.

Lynaia Jordan

"Hey Sun, we need to talk as soon as possible. So, when you get this message call me please."

I bet her and her husband is having a goodtime, well wait till this bubble gets busted."

Sun didn't call me back till the next day, I asked her if we could meet up and have lunch, I need to talk about something, she was cool with it.

"Melik and Earl I am going out for lunch, I will be back, we gonna need to talk when I get back cool?"

"Cool dad, did we do something?"

"Boy, no yall didn't do nothing, we will talk."

Last night I decided to tell them what I think and if what I think is true, Peaches is plotting to get Sun back and this is not gonna be pretty s we gotta be one step ahead of her.

"Hey Sun, did you order any drinks yet?"
"Yup, I figured this was a late lunch, so I got something light."
"Thanks Babe."
"So, Meth get right to it so I can eat."
"Right to what Sun."
"Right to what you asked me here for."

Lynaia Jordan

"Oh, so, you know I'm a nigga of my word and I can't sit around you and lie to you. Or even have your enemy laugh at you."

"Meth what do you mean my enemy, Peaches? How is this bitch laughing at me?"

"Well, don't you know the night of the reunion when I picked you up and I had to pick the money up over west?"

"Yeah, why? What do I have to do with that?"

"Let me finish Sun. So, I see your husband's car parked in the parking lot and I decide to turn around. Then once I started to think this is where Peaches use to hang at."

All I knew was that I had to pick her up off the floor. "Sun, Sun are you ok?"

"What, wait, what happened?"

She began to cry and trying to get up off the floor.

"Sun, stay there I called the ambulance, you need to get checked out."

"Meth, what I need you to do is leave me alone and stay out my life, I can't believe this shit."

She got up stormed out the restaurant and drove off, I kept calling her phone but no answer then eventually it started to go to voice mail.

"Man, what have I done, what have I done."

I need to talk to the boys, and it needs to be fast, before anything hit the fan and knowing Sun she is going straight to the source.

Lynaia Jordan

Chapter Twenty - Seven
Earl

"A Melik, I got a question do you think that your father hates our mother."

"Man, that's a crazy question, no he doesn't hate her."

"Why you ask that?"

"No reason man, it's just I'm not sure if I could trust your father after what he did to mommy."

"Earl, the stories I've heard from my family and my friends' mothers and fathers, our mother was rachet. She did mad shit to people that didn't deserve it, including your father. After you came my father said your father was a cool dude and before he told she your father you were his son she told my father first."

What, oh she wanna tell me what she wants me to know but not the whole truth, I can't trust her.

"Yo are you serious?"

"Yeah my father said he took care of you for a while until he found out you wasn't his and it was just a scheme for her to keep him away from Ms. Sun."

"Melik, I need your bro, you have to convince your father to let me to live her with yall please!"

"Done bro, but why, I thought you liked living with mommy."

Lynaia Jordan

"I really don't bro and it's not caused your father has money, it's because he is a real standup guy and I can trust him."

As me and Melik was talking, Mr. Meth walked in the door.

"A boy, I need to talk to yall one at a time, so Earl go up while I talk to Lek and if he decides to tell you later that's between yall."
"ok."

So, I just walked up the steps and stated to play the game. Melik must have done something bad, cause Meth face was twisted. About 30 minutes later Lek told me I can come down.

"Hey Earl, have a seat right here son."
"Meth could I go first please. Because I needed to talk to you anyway."
"Ok, go right ahead."
"First thing is I want to thank you for looking out for me because you didn't have to do it. Secondly, I wanted to know if I could come live with you and Melik permanently, third thing is, I know what kind of person my mother is, and she really hate Ms. Sun. She hates her so much that she got paid by Mr. Clyde to hook them up and her and Mr. Clyde dated. Oh, one other thing, Mr. Keith is trying to set yall up again, but this time he wants you."

Lynaia Jordan

Meth sat back in the chair and started to rub his head. He was so laid back and cool, He start his sentence off like this:

"Thank you, Earl, for being an honest young man, of course you can live with me, but I really need for you to continue to stay with Peaches until I figure out what to do. I need to know every move both of them make. I know this is a lot for you but your reward in the end is gonna be great. Just lay back cool and don't ever turn against me."
"I promise I won't."

"No since we got the easy stuff out the way, I need to make myself very clear with you. I love my children; I will die for my children. I know that Mee-Mee has a crush on and you and I know that you have pushed her off, time and time again and I also know that she is hard to resist, one reason is because she looks like her mother and the second is because she has my attitude. So, I want you to know she is off limits to you. Are we clear?"
"Crystal clear Meth."
"Good, we gonna be straight."

"Ok, thanks for everything seriously Meth."

So, he knows his daughter likes me and want to tell me to leave her alone. OK

Lynaia Jordan

Chapter Twenty - Eight
Sun

I can't believe that he just said that shit, I hate him, I hate Baltimore, I hate men, I hate Peaches. I can't do this anymore; I have to go.

"Ma, are you home, Hello Joy you in here?"
"Sun I'm here in the room."
"Ma what are you doing in here, I thought this was your junk room?"

"It is but I need to go through and clean out some of this junk."
"Ma you really hard stuff. Oh, my goodness looks at this lamp shade it's like something from the 50's."
"Yup you are right, this came from my mother's house when, I was a little girl, she told me that this was the first thing she brought when she moved out on her own. A lamp shade not even the lamp."
"Wow ma and you still have it, this something that we need to pass down from generation to generation."
"Sun the future will never be able to change or understand what we, they went through then so small things like this need to be able to be told throughout the family"
"Ma, I promise I will. I need your advice on something."
"Ok I'm all ears."

Lynaia Jordan

"Ok, so in so many words, Meth is trying to tell me that Peaches and Clyde knows each other."
"Ok, and what did he say to make you think that?"

"He said he seen Clyde's car at a bar that he knew Peaches use to hang out at."

"Sun Is that all the proof he has?
"Ma, he is right because I saw Clyde's car there that night when he was supposed to pick me up from the reunion, he turned his phone off ma."

"Sun the only think I am saying is know all the facts before you leap, you don't want to fall in a pit of shit without no rope and toilet paper!"

I had to laugh at that. My mother be real but the stuff that comes out her mouth.

"Ok ma, I understand so what should I say to him?"
"Alright, so you know he was there, but you don't know why, you know that Peaches use to go to this little neighborhood bar, so just ask him to go out and say you heard of this little place where the wings are good and the drinks are strong and see what he say when he pulls up."

"Ma you are so wise. It's like you know everything."
"I don't know everything, but I do know these damn bell bottom flowery pants need to go, I will keep the shirt tho."

I sat there for the rest of the evening helping my mother sort through clothes, papers, furniture and nail

198

polish to give away, this room was filled with a lot of my mother memories as a child, joy and mines as well.

Walking to my car, on my way home I noticed a black truck sitting in the middle of my mother block. I don't know but I got that funny feeling again. Let me hurry up home.

I waited a couple of more days before I asked Clyde to go out and I also avoided Meth throughout all of this, I do not want him clouding my mind. He just keeps leaving these messages on my voicemail.

"Hey Clyde, let's go out tonight?"
"Sure baby, what do you wanna do?"
"I wanna shoot some pool and have some drinks just chill for real."
"Oh yeah we can do that, get some wings and fries."
"Yeah Clyde something like that."
"Ok, we can go out tonight, let finish up some business and I will be back to get ready 9."
"That's cool I really need a break, dealing with the kids, my mother and everything else I wanna unwind!"
"Baby I noticed that you haven't sat down and relaxed since we been back to Baltimore."
"I know, that is getting ready to change we only have another month and then we have to take the twins back for school. I think that me, you and Meth needs to talk."

His face frowned up and he said, "Why do I need to talk to Meth again, please refresh my memory."

Lynaia Jordan

"Clyde, about him and his son coming to Georgia so he can be around the kids more. I am not moving back her."

"Oh that. Well baby I don't think that's a good idea. For our children or our marriage. It's no secret that he still loves you and in his fucked-up mind you are still his queen and yall are his family, I really don't want to have to kill him for fucking with me and that's that!"

I was shocked he really, this nigga just walked out the room. I wonder how he feels when we get in the car tonight!

Lynaia Jordan

Chapter Twenty- Nine
Clyde

What the fuck is this? I know this bitch then lost her mind. She is a fucking liar. I'm gonna kill her. I knew she was lying, she said that too fast and to nice. Then this bitch had a nerve to record us. I'm gonna kill her.

"Peaches, what the fuck is this Yo?"
"Nigga what do you mean?"
"The video you sent me?"
"Oh yeah just a little leverage just in case you want to act up. You liked it too, I can't lie, you are the best I ever had. I remember why Sun chose you over Meth, HaHa."
"Bitch, I'm gonna kill you, so fuck with me if you want delete this shit and don't call my fucking phone or don't text my phone. I'm done with ya snake as. You had me thinking that you changed."

"Oh, nigga please I am so tired of all your niggas saying you thought I changed, when will yall change. Everything that yall do have to revolve around her, my fucking kids, around her, my fucking men, around her, I can't even make a hair appointment on certain days because she I town. What the fuck Clyde. Yeah, but did you know that the same night this video had made her, and Meth was together."

"As a matter of a fact, she told me, and the reason that happened because you kidnapped me."

"I dint force you to drink, I only help you along while we were fucking because you, we drunk. Don't tell me I kidnapped you. I will be taking a test soon.!"

"What! Peaches, Hello!"

I know she didn't hang up on me, what the fuck she means a test, I'm gonna kill this bitch, I mean it. I need to call my man.

"Hey Percy, can you talk man?"
"Yeah, what sup?"
"Man, I think I messed up Yo."
"Clyde what happened?"
"Percy, I got drunk and fucked my ex."
HaHaHa "Boy that's not a fuck up unless she pregnant."
"She recorded it and she said she gonna get test. I have to tell Sun the truth she will understand."
"Ok, relax, if she takes a test you still have nine months before you tell ya wife. Where do she have the video?"
"I think on her phone."
"Ard, you gotta get with her again and take her phone. Once you get it erase all content in it. Hopefully she doesn't back up often."

"She probably doesn't even know how."

Lynaia Jordan

"Ok, if not let's do that first then call me back, I might come up cause the we need to meet for a briefing."

"Ok, got you anytime, let me know you can stay at my mother's house."

"Fam take it easy see you soon."

I am so glad that I have someone I can reach out to. He def gonna help me get back under control.

"Sun, I'm on my way, could you have me something out to wear?"

"Ok, Clyde, I'm ready."

Got home put my clothes on and we were out.

"So, Sun where would you like to go?"

"Well that night of the reunion, Meth took me to this little whole in the wall over west, Lets go there it was mad cars outside, we didn't go in because he said the guy wasn't there. I know where it is."

"Ok, let's go"

As we were driving, I didn't realize that she was taking me my bar. Yo, what the fuck! She seen the video, she knows, but she so calm. I don't know what to do. I gotta think, what to do. Peaches might be here or anything. I snuck and texted Percy 911 when we stopped for gas. He called.

"Hello."

"Yo you good 911."

Lynaia Jordan

"Naw you, whats wrong no problem, I will call you when I get there."

"What nigga what are you talking about."

"It's ok Percy you my man, I got ya back."

I hung that phone up so fast and Sun was like.

'Baby is everything ok?"

"Sun don't be upset honey, I just have to give us a raincheck on the pool and wings. Percy need me."

"I'm good baby, we all have to do what we have to do. I'm good. Just get me something to eat before I go in."

"You are the best; I will make it up to you."

Once I dropped off Sun, I called peaches and told her to meet me at the hotel we were at.

Chapter Thirty
Earl

"Ma, let me show this text message the daughter sent me."

"Earl, she is a little fast one, we got her. I won't even have to use Clyde."

"Ma what you want me to do?"
"Nothing right now let me get this together."
"Ok"

Her phone went off, and it was Clyde. She said, "Oh this nigga wants to meet me tonight, guess he scared, I want you to come with me and sit in the car, because he threatened me."

"Ok, let me go put my hoodie on."
"Yeah, put ya hoodie on so he won't know it's you. You are just like your father, the strongest man I knew."

When we arrived at the Marriott she parked where I can see him pull in, he got there like 30 minutes after her.

"Hello, Meth"

"Yeah whats good Earl."

Lynaia Jordan

"Clyde just met my mother at the Marriott Hotel downtown, I don't know the floor, but she said she needed me to go with her because he threatened her."

"That's fine we good, this is all I need."
"Ok, I will give you an update later."
"Ok, I got something special for you tomorrow, come over."
"No problem I will be there like 12 if that's ok?"
"Yeah that's good, thanks again Earl."

When I hung of the phone, I decided to text Mee-Mee to see whats she is doing.

Earl: Mee-Mee what you doing?
Mee-Mee: Who is this stop playing with me Melik.
Earl: It's me, wyd.
Mee-Mee: Nothing, over here chilling with these girls off my grandmother block. Why wyd?
Earl: I'm sitting in a car waiting for my mother to come out of this place. I need to tell you something.
Mee-Mee: What?
Earl: Your father knows that you like me.

Texts stopped after that she didn't even respond no more so I just left it alone.

It's been like two hours and no Clyde or my mother. Let me text her.
Earl: Ma what's up?

Lynaia Jordan

Ma: I'm good, will be done in like 10 minutes.
    Earl: Ma it's been two hours.
Ma: Bye Earl here I come.

She hung the phone up. About 20 minutes later I seen Clyde coming and getting into his car. This time I took a picture.

"Hmmm Just in case I need some proof."

Let me call Meth and let him know I got pictures.

Lynaia Jordan

Chapter Thirty-One
Peaches

Yes, I got him, we are going to be together. Last week was amazing. I need to cut Keith off, but I need to keep him close. You know what I'm just gonna tell Meth what I know and let him handle it.

"Hello Meth"
"What Peaches?"
"Look I need to meet and talk to you for a second about some real important shit."
"Ard you know where I am, I will be here till 7."
"Ok, I'm on my way."

When I turned around Keith was standing right there in the door way listening.

"So, what do you need to talk to Meth about that you can't say over the phone?"

"Well since you must know it's about his daughter liking Earl and I had a talk with Earl, so he needs to talk to his daughter."

"Oh shit! Yeah, we don't need that to go down, it's gonna be some shit. Sun not having that, No form or fashion."

Lynaia Jordan

This nigga was laughing all goofy like it was so funny.

"Ard Keith, I will be back like around 7."

It killed me to give this nigga a kiss, but I got to play the part just until I talk to Meth.

I walked into the car wash and Meth was sitting there waiting for me.

"Hey Meth"

"Whats up Peaches."

"Well, first thing is your little daughter like my son, second thing is Keith is trying to get you. He has an investigation around us. I guess he believe that you are still running drugs out of here. I think that you need to lay low really quick."

He stood up and leaned over his desk, his hand started to ball, and he started to get that look.

"Peaches, what did you tell this nigga about me?"

"Nothing Meth, I promise."

"You better had not. Now aint shit in here and honestly aint shit going on, but we gonna make him think it is."

Meth started to laugh, here is what you gonna do.

Lynaia Jordan

"I got you this time plus you owe me for fucking with Sun husband."

"What, Boy please I don't even know that nigga like that.   Whatever you thinking you need to stop, you just trying to get Sun back."

"That's true and you and he is true too but I aint telling, I don't give a damn about him, its gonna come out!"

"Whatever, I'm moving out his house this weekend, I'm telling him tonight, I can't fuck with him and as long as we aint doing nothing wrong we should be good."

I walked out the office and he yelled out "A Peaches you are looking a little phat back there.!"

"Nigga please you will never hit this again."

I made to Keith's house; I am so glad that I didn't let go of my place.

"Keith baby come here."
"Peaches whats up."
"Keith, I have mad love for you, but this is not working."
"What, girl you crazy."
"Keith listen, we are from two different worlds, my son doesn't like you and I can't see myself spending the rest of my life with you."

Lynaia Jordan

He sat down, I guess that took him by surprise he thought he had me.

"I will have me and Earl things out by the end of the week. I just can't do this anymore."

"Peaches is it someone else? How can I change? You want me to retire, I can."

Oh, he is playing this role good. "No Keith I just want you to be happy and move on with your life."

I walked out the living room and I was laughing so hard in the inside.

Lynaia Jordan

Chapter Thirty-Two
Meth

Peaches called me to help her move. I was cool with that, because I really wanted to see where this nigga Keith lives, in case I have to do something to him.

"Meth can you grab that bag right there?"

"Damn Peaches how much stuff did you move in here?"

"I know Meth it just piled up, but this is the last of it."

"I hope so cause I'm tired."

Once we pulled off from Keith's house, I noticed a black SUV following us. I called Peaches.

"Hey Peaches, do you see that black SUV following us."

"Yeah, that's just Keith making sure I get to my house safe. I have been seeing that truck since I got home."

"Peaches you not worried, just in case it's not Keith."

"Meth who else would it be. You are tripping."

"ok whatever. I'm tired probably."

"Yeah you tired but you can't sleep at my house."

Once I dropped Peaches stuff off, I didn't see the SUV again. I headed home.

Man, this summer is going by fast.

Lynaia Jordan

Chapter Thirty-Three
Earl

"Hello"

"E you alone"

"yeah whats up"

"Is everything in place?"

"I got it, just waiting for the right time. You ready, cause once we do this It's no turning back."

"I'm ready, did you tell your mother your plan?"

"No, I don't think I can trust her, she still loves Meth and she wants to make Sun pay so her vision is clouded. She apart of the problem too,"

"What about Malik?"

"Don't worry about Malik he gonna be just fine. He is not a problem. I got to go them coming in the house."

"Whats Up Earl"

"Hey Meth, thanks for helping my mother getting our stuff, I got everything in place so this gonna take no time."

"Yeah, I'm just dropping off then headed home cause IM tired."

"Oh ard, just sit it all in the Livingroom, is it cool if I come over this evening once I'm done."

"Let me see if the twins there or not. I will hit you and let you know."

"Meth you don't have to worry about me and Mesha, I'm good, I wouldn't disrespect you like that."

"I know Earl but I gotta make sure."

Lynaia Jordan

"Ok, just hit me and let me know."

Once he left, I helped my mother organize the house.

"Ma, I'm going out, I will hit you once I get back."

"Earl, where you are going, I wanted to cook dinner."

"I wanted to hoop up with some friends get some pizza or something."

"Ok, do you have our key?"

"yeah, I won't be out to late."

Walking out the door I knew that I had to get things straight fast cause she really is trying to play the mother role. I think it's a little too late for that.

"Fool whats good."

"Where you at man, I been sitting in this truck for an hour."

"Look, you do what I say."

"E why you always gotta go there?"

"Nigga because I can, and aint shit nobody gonna do about it, now move over so I drive."

"You don't care if anyone see you driving this truck."

"No, I'm just gonna say it's yours. How did you do today with Sun."

"Well, she stayed at her mother's house pretty much all day, the kids were in and out."

"Ok. good let's get over to the house, somehow I gotta convince her daughter to meet me here."

"Yo you know that she gonna be down for anything her little dumb ass, we should run a train on her."

Lynaia Jordan

I just smacked the shit out of this dumb nigga."

"If I ever hear you talk about her like that again I'm going to kill you."

"what you got feeling for her, she is a youngin, yo, and why you hit me man, you could have told me to not say that again I would have listened."

"Shut the hell up with ya cry baby ass. I got to try and figure this out."

Lynaia Jordan

Chapter Thirty-Four
Sun

I never thought that she wasn't going to make through the summer. The beginning of the summer was the best time I ever had with my mother. She was in remission and out of nowhere she was gone. I had to say strong for Joy and the twins. I knew my mother my whole life and now she is gone. I need to take a walk; I need some air. When I turned and started to walk out the room Clyde came behind me to see if I was ok.

"Clyde I'm fine I just need a little bit of air baby; I will be right back."

"Ard call me if you need me to come outside with you."
"Ok"

Walking out of the hospital was like walking out of oxygen less chamber. I couldn't breathe or hear anything in there. I was numb and my heart hurt so badly. No one could comfort me because I didn't want to be comforted. Deep down inside the only thing I wanted was for my mother to wake up and tell me that she was ok. I know that I haven't been a going to church lately, but I do know that it is a God and he is watching over me. With my face full of tears, I walked towards my car only to find Meth standing there with his butt on the hood of my car.

"How did you hear?"
"Mee-Mee called me. Sun I am so sorry, if there is anything, I can do for you and the kids just let me know."

All I could do was call out his name "Meth!" I looked him in his eyes and saw into his soul. I could see was love for me.

"Meth she is gone. I don't have a mother anymore. She was my mother." The tears wouldn't stop falling and all he could do was grab me and hold me.

Whispering in my ear he said "Sun, it's going to be ok, I know how you feel baby; I am here for you and always will be no
matter what."

He held me for a few more minutes. His touch gave me comfort and at that moment all my pain went to love. I knew Meth had my heart; he will have my heart forever. No matter how far I try to run, I can't forget about the way he makes my heart feel.

"Sun you have to get it together and take care of your mother for the last time."

Lynaia Jordan

When he said that it sent chills over my body, but he was right this will be the last time I will be able to take care of my mother. I gave Meth a hug and said "Thank you for everything"

I turned to walk back to the hospital and knew I had to do this last thing for my mother. Walking in the room Joy and Clyde were still standing there looking at my mother's lifeless body. I walked over to the bed and touched Joy's shoulder and said, "Come on Joy we need to get things together for mommy."

Joy turned to me with so much hurt and pain in her eyes. "What! What Sun! You want to hurry up and put her away nice so you and your family can go back to yall nice house and live yall amazing life like mommy didn't even die. Well you go right ahead I am going to stay right here as long as I can."

She laid across my mother's body and cried out. I couldn't do anything but stand there and cry too. I went over to Joy and
grabbed her.

"Sis I love you with all my heart. I love mommy too and
always will. Yall loved me before anyone did. I didn't turn my back Joy, yall acted like it was cool I wanted to leave. I am going to be here with you as long as you need me. You are my sister and I love you."

Lynaia Jordan

We sat in the hospital room for another hour and then they said we had to leave. I told Clyde I was going back to my mother's house. The kids wanted to go with his mother, so he was going to take them there and then come back to my mother's house with me.

"Hey twins come and give me a hug. I love you both with all my heart. Are yall ok?"

"Yes ma" said Mee-Mee "Yeah Ma, I'm good as long as you are ok."

"I'm fine Junior. I will see yall in the morning. I love yall"

Clyde came in my face and said, "Are you ok baby?"

"Clyde I am ok, I guess it really haven't hit me yet. When I get to my mother's house I am going to walk to the bar and get me a drink. I know all of the family will be there in the morning. I just don't want to be bothered with people right now. I know that drinking is not going to make the pain go away but I want a
drink tonight."

"That's fine baby I will be there to sip with you later, but you call me sooner if you need me. I love you Sun."

"Love you too Clyde, see you later."
The whole ride home Joy didn't say a word to me, and I didn't bother her cause I really feel some kind of way about what Joy said in the hospital room, but I know she is

Lynaia Jordan

hurting so I am not going to dwell on it. I got out the car and started to walk down the block and Joy went in the empty house. When I got to the corner of my mother's block, I heard a familiar sound. I turned around only to find Meth sitting in his car making a sound like he was calling a cat.

"Hey, do you need a ride?" I smiled "No thank you, I am going right here to the bar then going back to my mother's house."

"Oh, ok, well you have a nice night young lady."

Then he pulled off. I walked into the bar and ordered a fifth of goose and two bottles of pineapple juice. When I got back to my mother's house, I noticed that same black truck parked down the street, I hurried in there, opened the door and Meth was there sitting on the living room sofa.

"What are you doing here Mr.?"
"Well, I called Junior to make sure yall was ok and he told me they were with Clyde staying at his moms' house tonight."

You should have seen his face when he said that." So, Sun, what are you drinking?"

"Goose and Pineapple juice."
"Ard, well Sun you want to take a drink with me?"
I smiled at him and said, "Of course I do."

220

Lynaia Jordan

I walked into the kitchen to get the glasses because I know this was going to be a long night. I walked back to the living room and Meth was sitting on the floor looking through my mother photo album books.

"Do you like what you are looking at?"

He looked up and said, "I love what I am looking at!"

"Whatever Meth let's drink and talk about my mother because when Clyde come you know you are going to want to leave."

"Sun I'm not leaving your side tonight! So, let's drink."

We looked over my baby pictures first. Meth thought it was so funny to see me in my birthday suit. He saw pictures of me mother when she was younger. In amazement he stated, "Wow Sun you look just like your mother she was beautiful!"

I didn't say anything; I just turned the page to the next picture. I felt him looking in my face. So, I wanted to cut the tension. The

Next picture was of me and Meth at our baby's shower.

"How time flies, you were the most beautiful pregnant woman I have ever seen."

"Aww Meth you are just saying that because I was pregnant
with your twins."

"No Sun seriously, you know how some women noses get wide and their necks get black. None of that

Lynaia Jordan

happened to you. Sun the only thing that happened to you was that you got stretch marks and your feet swelled."

I gave him a look but we both couldn't do anything but laugh.
 Over the next three hours we drank, and I tried calling Clyde
like seven times but it went straight to voice mail. Before I knew it I was drunk.
"Come on Meth, let's play a game?"
'What kind of game you have in mind Sun."
"Well let's play strip horse. Remember how we use to play
horse in front of my mother's door. Well this time you have to lay down and make the shots on Juniors old toy basketball hoop." Looking at the hoop I remember my mother calling me
telling me she had bought him that hoop so when he comes to visit, he will have something to play with. Meth sat there and thought about it for a second and then he laid back on the floor and said, "Bring it on baby I'm ready!"

"Ok, let me lock the door and then let the games began."
Meth really thought he was going to win. I know he is going to play hard so he can see me naked. The first couple of shots we both made. Then things started to turn around and before I knew it, I was in my panties and he was in his boxers.

Lynaia Jordan

"Meth I am getting ready to end this now. This shot is going to with my left hand and my eyes closed."

"What come on Sun, I am drunk."

"Look do you want to play or take something off?"

"I'm playing now let me see you make this shot, because if you don't the next one, I shoot will be impossible."

So, I had to get myself together. This was going to be a hard shot, but I know I could do it. Telling myself Come on Sun get your eye on the hoop and throw. I closed my eyes and I threw the ball. The living room was so quite you could hear a penny drop or better yet the swish sound when a ball goes through the hoop.

"Oh my god, I can't believe you made that shot."

"Well believe it Mr. Meth!"

I was clapping my hands and everything because I knew it was only luck that I made that shot.

"Ok so now it's your turn to shoot, you know if you miss you have to take off your underwear."

I must admit, I really wanna see what it's is down there now been a lot of years.

"Come on Sun you gonna make me take this shot?"

"Hell yeah, you got me laying here with my panties on"

I saw him holding that ball in his hands, he was ready to throw it when my phone rung. I hopped up and answered it.

Lynaia Jordan

"Hello"
"Hey baby is you ok? You were trying to call me, but I fell
a sleep."

"Yeah, I was just making sure yall was ok. You never
came here, where are the kids?"

"Sun we are ok, the twins are sleep. Sun, I don't feel
like coming all the way over there. I am exhausted, it's
nothing we can do tonight. I will be there in the morning
with the kids. Are you and Joy ok tonight?"

"I understand Clyde, your tired, we good I will just
see yall in the morning. I have to meet the funeral director
in the morning."

"Ok baby we will be there like 10. I'm gonna give
you enough time to get yourself together cause you sound
fucked up."
I laughed a little cause he was right. "Yeah Clyde I'm drunk
for sure."

"Goodnight baby, I love you."
"Love you too Clyde."

I hung the phone up but holding it in my hand
because I was glad, he wasn't coming, but confused on my
other feeling. I wanted to spend more time with Meth. As
I was walking to the living room, I seen that the lights were
cut off. I couldn't see anything going into the living room.
In a quiet voice I called his name. "Meth, Meth are you in
here."

Lynaia Jordan

Maybe he left. Damn!

I turned around to turn the lights on and I could smell his cologne. He was standing right in front of me breathing hard. It was only a little of light coming down the stairs from the hallway window, so I went and stood in it. I could hear Meth walking over to me until I finally saw his naked body standing in front of me.

"Why are you naked Meth, you didn't even take the shot."

"Oh, but Sun I did, and I missed it, so you won. Now in all fairness I had to let you see what you won."

He started to walk closer to me, and I began to back up because I was really scared of what I was going to do when he touched me. His dick was rock hard. Since I wasn't paying attention I bumped into the stairs. When I lifted my head up, he was right there on me. He put his face right in mine. He kissed my lips oh so softly, I tried to resist but I couldn't. I missed his soft lips. He began to rub the head of his dick between my legs. Once I felt that I was flowing like a river.

"Wait, Meth I don't have a condom and we need one."

"Sun, I don't have one either."

At this point I was ready to stop. The next thing I knew he was on his knees between my legs. Making my

225

body feel like It was my first time. I moaned "Wait Meth, Please Wait!"

With his mouth full he mumbled "Sun please baby, I can't I have to have you. Please just let go and relax, I promise you, I won't hurt you."

I lifted his head up and looked him in his eyes and he had me. He picked me up and carried to my room. Opening the door with his back. Meth laid me on my bed. Pulling my panties off with his mouth he licked the inner of my thighs, turned me over and began to massage my ass. I knew what was coming next. He licked my ass like it was a sweet slice of watermelon on a hot summer day. When he put himself inside of me, I melted all over him. I couldn't really believe we were here together making love again. It was wonderful. After we were finish, I went into the bathroom and looked at myself in the mirror. At that moment I saw a woman who let her guard down and because of my weakness I am an adulterer. I made love to the man that had my heart and I betrayed the man that loved me unconditionally.
The next morning when I woke up, I had a purple rose on my pillow with a note:

Dear Sun,
I watched you sleep all night and the only words you kept saying was you were sorry. I feel so bad that I love you so much. I know what we did last night was wrong, but Sun I love you and always will and whenever you think the time

Lynaia Jordan

is right for us, I will be waiting for you. You will forever be
my soulmate. Once you read this destroy it because I have
already caused enough pain to you.
Forever your King,
Meth

I jumped out of the bed to notice it was only eight thirty. This gave me enough time to get myself together. I ran me a nice hot bubble bath, walking past my mother's room to see if Joy was in there and she must have been already gone. Laying back in the tub reminiscing on what happened last night and how I now lust for a man that is not my husband but is the father of my children. I just soaked there for a little while. Once I got out the tub I walked to my room and Joy was sitting on my bed.

"Good Morning Joy."

She turned to look at me and said "Is it really, Bitch do you think I am having a good morning. We lost our mother yesterday and all you have on your selfish ass mind is getting back with Meth."

"That's not true Joy, I know mommy wouldn't want us to be all sad and crying over her."

"Sun how in the hell do you know what she wanted. You left us, the first chance you got. You packed you precious little twins up and started a new life somewhere

227

else. Mama was up suffering and always worried about you and your babies. Her precious Sun! I took care of her. No, she didn't want for anything because you made sure we had money but Love you didn't give us any! Oh, but I know your little secret and it makes me feel so much better to know that you are not perfect.

Today I want to make funeral arrangements for my mother. It will be what I want! After the funeral and her will is read, I want you to leave, I don't need you here. If you were here when she really needed you, she might still be here."

The look that Joy had in her eye it just hurt my soul, I couldn't say anything cause when I think back over the years, I wasn't here emotionally for them. I know that my little sister blames me for our mother dying. I know she has to blame something but why me. Once Joy was finishing saying all of that she got up off my bed and walked out my room. I just sat there and cried because maybe she is right, I am selfish.

Lynaia Jordan

Chapter Thirty-Five
Clyde

You know hanging up the phone with Sun, something in my soul just didn't sit right. I tossed and turned for a little while until I had to go and be with my wife. She needed me. I looked at the clock and it read 4:30, by time I get there it will be five and the sun will be coming up. When I turned on the block, I saw Meth pulling off. I just sat there, hurt, confused, and heart broken. I knew she was drunk but not enough to be with him. A feeling went through my body, I sat there and let the situation run through my head for a minute then I went back to my mother's house to get the kids.

I decided to go for a run first before I went back into the house with the kids. It seems like ran for hours. I left my cell phone in the car. After a while I decided to head back home. I really don't know what happened. I am going to confront Meth not my wife. If he thinks he can have her back he is mistaken, I will do whatever it takes to keep my family and if that means taking Meth out the picture then so be it. Walking into the house I was greeted by the kids.

"Hey Clyde, did you go and get mommy yet or did you go for your morning workout?"

Lynaia Jordan

"I went for my morning workout Junior but get dressed and we can go pick her up and go to breakfast ask my mother would she like to go as well."

My inner feelings won't let me shake the thoughts of her and him. I took a quick shower. I had to think about a few things. Did Sun know about me and Peaches? Did Meth tell her? Did my wife sleep with her ex? I don't know my mind is going crazy and I only can blame myself. When we pulled up to Sun's mother house she was sitting outside on the steps. I got out the car and walked over to her and gave a hug and a kiss.

"Hey sweetie, are you ok?"
"Yes, Clyde I am fine. Did you and the kids sleep well last night?"
"Yes, we did. I thought about you though all night. I was wondering if you were ok. I know this is a difficult time for you right now."
I see Junior and Mee-Mee walking up to their mother, so I stopped the conversation we were having.
"Ma, are you ok?" asked Junior
"Yes, baby I am ok, I love you so much."

She walked over and gave him a big hug.
"Mee-Mee come give mommy a hug."

Mee-Mee gave Sun a hug, but she had a look on her face when she stepped back.

Lynaia Jordan

"Well come on let's go inside, the funeral home is gonna be here any minute to talk to me and aunt Joy."

When I walked in the house I saw where they were sitting because it was still two cups on the table. Sun walked over to pick up the two cups and I said, "Baby have a seat let me get this for you."

She had a weird look on her face. Right then and there I knew that they did something.
"So, you and Joy were in here drinking last night?"
"Yeah, we kind of got a little drunk but, I don't have a hangover and neither does she."

I am not going to ask her anymore questions I am just going to go straight to the source Meth. I am going to wait until the funeral was over to approach him. Joy walked through the door with a frown on her face looked at Sun rolled her eyes then came into the kitchen with me and the kids.

"Hey Joy, how are you feeling today?"
"Clyde, I feel terrible, it so sad. I lost everything yesterday Clyde."

Joy began to cry, and it was my instinct to grab her and hold her comfort her.

"Joy, I may not know a lot, but I know enough. You are strong and you will make it through, and we will be here for you. Me, the kids and Sun."

231

Lynaia Jordan

She lifted her head up off my shoulder and she looked at me and nodded ok. I looked at my watch and it was quarter to eleven. Almost time for the funeral director to be there.

"Hey Sun, do you want me to take the kids out for lunch while yall conduct business or do you want me to be here?"

"No Clyde, I want you here with me Meth is on his way to get the kids. He has something planned for them today."

"Oh, ok, well let me let them know and I will be right back."

I walked in the kitchen when someone rang the doorbell.
It was Meth, I was heated but I couldn't let it show.
Sun got up and answered the door and told him to come in.

"Morning everyone" Meth spoke as he walked through the doors. I didn't even get a chance to tell the kids but that's ok. I turned back around and walked into the living room. He was standing by Sun whispering something.

"Umm, they are ready Sun."
"Ok, well Meth thanks for getting the kids today. Call and let us know how yall making out, ok."

Lynaia Jordan

"Sure Sun, but we should be good. Do you want me to bring them back here or drop them off at Clyde's?"

"We will call you." Said Sun
"Hey Meth, do you need any money for them?" I said sarcastically.

He laughed a little and then said "Naw, we should be good. Thanks for asking though."

It took everything in me not to knock this nigga out. I kept my cool. Gave my kids a hug and a kiss told them I loved them, and I would see them later. When they were leaving out the door the funeral director was coming in. I sat there held my wife hand and listen to her and her sister make arrangements for their mother. When they were finish Joy got up and ran out the house.

"Sun are you really ok baby."
"No, Clyde, I am hurting inside, I am dying inside. I don't know what reality is. I can't explain the feelings I have. I just don't know"
"Baby it will be ok, and whatever it is we can work through it, anything Sun."
She hugged and kissed me so tight. I thought she was getting ready to tell me at that moment, but she didn't she just asked me if I wanted to go get something to eat. We got in the car while driving down the street we seen Joy sitting on the corner crying and talking to herself.

233

Lynaia Jordan

"Sun you need to talk to your sister. She is going through something."

"Clyde, I didn't tell you, but Joy blames me for mommy's death. She feels if I was here, she would have not gotten so sick. I don't know what to say to her."

"Sun you have to keep talking to her and just be there for her. Every step of the way. Baby go head I have a few things to do and I will be at my mom's house afterwards. Take ya sister out, yall do some stuff together. I love you Sun so much and call me if you need me."

"Ok, baby thank you so much for everything. Love you."

"Love you too Sun."

When I pulled off, she walked towards her sister. I need someone to talk to fast before I explode. Let me call Percy he is the only person I can talk to.

"Hello" Percy answered the phone like he was out of breath.

"Hey man, I need you to come up. It's time."

"Say no more, I'm on my way."

The line went dead and I'm not sure about what I'm about to do. But it gotta be done.

Lynaia Jordan

Chapter Thirty-Six
Meth

All I could think about was the other night, it was amazing, I knew she still loved me. I don't feel bad either, cause that nigga is still fucking Peaches.

"Dad, is everything ok with Mee-Mee and Junior?"

"Yeah Melik, they are fine, we have to be there for them on Saturday."

"Ok, you know I have never been to a funeral before."

"Yeah, I know."

"Can I go over Ms. Sun house tomorrow and chill with them"

"Let me call her and ask her. Melik we may be moving to Georgia when they go back down there."

"Seriously, I'm glad because we really have started a good relationship, I'm gonna miss my mother but I will just act like she locked up."

"Boy, you crazy!"

"Seriously"

My phone rung and it was an unknown number.

"Hello"

"Meth it's me Clyde, I need to holla at you."

"Ok, where and when."

"We can wait til after the funeral, at the Car Wash is cool."

Lynaia Jordan

"You sure you wanna wait?"

"Yeah, I'm sure, Sun is already going through enough, I don't need her worrying about us talking."

"Ok, talk to you then."

This nigga hung the phone up and honestly, I don't care if he knew about me and Sun or not. Let me call her to make sure she aint say nothing.

"Sun, I need to ask you a question."

"Hello Sun, how are you? Oh, hey Meth I'm doing a little better today."

"Sun, I'm sorry. How are you?"

"I'm doing ok, whats up?"

"Well ya husband called me today."

"For what Meth."

"He said he need to talk to me. You didn't tell him, did you?"

"No, but before my other passed, I did tell him we needed to talk about you and Melik moving to Georgia."

"Oh ok, that's probably it then."

"Ard, so I'm gonna see you and Melik on Saturday, yeah we wouldn't miss it for the world, you need me to do anything or get anything?"

"You could get the chicken if you want, because my cousin said she gonna cook 200 pieces and I aint feeling that."

I laughed a little cause her cousin can't cook but always wanting to.

Lynaia Jordan

"I got the chicken."

"Thanks, Meth, for everything."

"You know you are always welcomed, and I will do anything for you, I love you."

"I know, Dido"

She hung the phone up, I was surprised at the dido, but I already knew that. She was my destiny from the first time I saw her. My world my everything. I finally have her back.

Lynaia Jordan

Chapter Thirty-Seven
Clyde

"Percy, thanks for coming man. I know you had to get everything in order down there."

"Man listen, we good, so whats going on?"

"I saw some shit that fucked my head up."

"Damn nigga what did you see."

"Meth, coming for Sun mothers house at 5 it the morning."

"Yo, that's crazy, but I thought it was Peaches for real."

"Naw, Yo for real I been sleeping with her on the regular, that's the only thing that keeps her in check, I figured we are leaving in like two weeks anyway so fuck it."

"So, you worried about Meth and fucking Peaches?"

"Yeah, my wife loved him yo."

"Man, so you want me to eliminate Meth?"

"No, I want you to be with me while I talk to him."

This nigga laughed in my face.

"What you scared of this nigga."

"Come on Yo, just want it to look intimidating to him, that's all. I aint never scared,"

"Yeah ard, whatever, I'm staying at your mother's house?"

"Yeah, come on you here for Suns mother funeral."

We drove over to the house.

Lynaia Jordan

"Yo ya mother house big as shit."
    Yeah, she did good for herself."
"You aint buy this for her?"
    "No!"
"Ok, I like ya moms."
I had to give this nigga a look.

    "What, she looks good too so don't try shit!"
"Oh, I can't holla at ya mother?"
    "What nigga"
"Sike Clyde, I'm just joking."

    "Baby, Sun, I'm back."
She came down the looking so beautiful.

    "Hey, baby, Oh Percy you here."
"Yes Sun, I'm so sorry about you mother."
    "Percy, thank you, just want Saturday to come and go."
"I know, I had to bury my mother as well."
    "Wow, I didn't know that."
"Yeah, I don't talk about it much, but it was very hard, support from family and friends always helped."
    "Yeah, it does make it easier Percy but thank you."
"You are welcomed Sun."
    "Babe, I'm gonna talk to Percy for a second, we probably go to the gym and get a couple of drinks if that is ok."

Lynaia Jordan

"Clyde, don't be silly that is fine, I am going to the mall so that I can get a couple of things."
"Ok call me if you need me., will the kids be home today?"
"No, they are coming tomorrow. I will call Meth to see whats they are up to though."
"Ok, Love you."
"Love you too Clyde."

I watched my wife as she walked out the door, she has a lot on her and the shit I involved in not gonna help any.

"Hey Percy thanks man, look at this shit."
I showed him the video
"Yo what the fuck you do? This shit gonna kill her, she lost her mother now her husband to her enemy. This is bad."
"I know yo, she drugged me, her same M.O. when she would get niggas got. I don't know why the fuck I thought I could trust her."
"Well now we got to figure out a way to make this go away. I think I got an idea."
"Yo help me out please. I can't hurt Sun, that's all people do to her has hurt her."
"I got you Clyde, I gotta scope shit out for a second, take me around and let me meet these clown ass Baltimore people."
"let's go workout first then get some drinks."

Lynaia Jordan

Chapter Thirty-Eight
Sun

Momma looked so pretty; the service was good. The pastor talked about my mother like he knew her all his life. I'm hurting so bad because my children will never be able to know the mother, I knew as a grandmother. I had Meth and Clyde right by myside. As they were carrying the cast out the church, I saw the same black truck across the street and this time, I got a good look at the driver. I don't know who he is.

"Clyde, baby."
"Whats wrong baby, are you ok, it's gonna be ok."
"No Clyde that is the truck I keep seeing, it has been following me around the whole summer. Something is not right."
Clyde looked across the street and seen the truck, but the person rolled the window up. He called Percy and Meth. They all looked over there, Meth came over to me.
"Sun come with me, I seen this truck before something is going on."
"No Meth this is my mother's funeral and whatever you have going on I don't want to be a part of it"

He gave me a look of hurt.

Lynaia Jordan

"Sun you really think I would put you and my kids in danger at your mother's funeral. This don't have shit to do with me, maybe it has something to do with your lying ass husband. You know what maybe all these years I thought I loved you and I got a second chance at love with you, I'm done!"

What just happened. I looked over at Clyde and he kept saying he was sorry. What is happening.

"Clyde whats happening? What is Meth talking about?"
"Sun, baby, I don't know what he is talking about."
"I won't do this here, but we need to talk."
"Ok baby, let me see whats up with this truck."
"Clyde Fuck that truck, I'm burying my mother today and then we are heading home, Joy don't want me here, and I'm so done with Baltimore."

I walked to the twins took their hand and got into the family car. I didn't see Meth at the burial or repast.

"Ma can I sit out front for a second I need some air."

"Yes, MeeMee don't walk off we going to be leaving in a minute."
"Ok, I won't love you ma. I'm sorry this happened to you."
"Baby, this GOD's doing its nothing you should be sorry for but thank you for loving me."

Lynaia Jordan

I watched my daughter walk outside, then I saw Earl leave out right behind her. A couple people walked up to me and before I could step outside to see whats going on Mee-Mee was gone.

"Meth, whats Earls number Mee-Mee is gone with him."

"Wait what! I am calling him right now I'm on my way over there."

"Excuse me did you see my daughter and a dark-skinned young man sitting out here?"

"Yeah the pulled off in a black SUV."
Screaming "CLYDE, PERCY, CLYDE"

"Sun whats wrong baby why are you screaming like that?"

"Ma whats wrong?"
"Junior whats Earl's phone number?"

"I don't know I will ask Malik."
"Clyde, Percy he took my baby."

"Sun   who   took   her?"
"Clyde it was Earl. It was Earl the whole time."

"Who Peaches son Earl"
"Yes, Clyde he has MeeMee. She asked me could she go sit outside and I told her yes, then I saw him leave out. So, I came out to see what was up and they were gone, people said they left in a black SUV. Clyde please find her."

Clyde gave me a hug and said "Sun, I will find her."
"Come on Percy lets go. Sun I will be back."

Lynaia Jordan

Meth Pulled up.

"Sun, are you ok?"

"No Meth he has her, my stomach is telling me this is not good."

"I knew it was so crazy that Peaches son came back just like that. He not answering his phone."

"Meth please find out little girl. Please."
"I will, I'm calling Peaches right now, I'm just gonna head over to their house."

"I am coming too Meth."
"No Sun, you need to stay her with junior."

"Meth, I am coming. Joy, can you watch Junior please and let me know if they come back. I am so sorry Joy."

"Aint nothing new everything has to be about you anyway but go and find my niece."
"Junior I will be back call Malik and see if he talked to Earl."

It was silencing the whole ride to Peaches house.

Lynaia Jordan

Chapter Thirty-Nine
Earl

"Yo what are you doing I said wait at the mother's house. They saw you."

"Naw, I rolled the window up."

"Nigga just meet me at Suns' mother house."

"Ard, I will be there."

I hung up the phone this has to work, they gonna pay a lot money for her.   These motherfuckers owe me for everything I went through and lost in my life.   They took my mother away from me and my father.   If they want her back, they gonna pay.

"Mee-Mee lets go outside and talk."

"Ard let me ask my mother you know how she is."

"Ard once I see you walk out; I will leave out too."

"Ok."

I saw her walk out the house, so I followed her.   No one even expected.

"Mee are you ok?"

"Yeah, it's just a little sad to see my mother hurting."

"Yeah, I know that hurting feeling."

"I'm sorry, I forgot you loss your father."

"It's ok, I am so tired of seeing people cry."

Lynaia Jordan

"Me too."
"MeeMee you want to go hang out with me and my boy."
I don't think that is a good idea. My mother might need me."
"Mee when are you gonna stop acting like a baby. I got you, I got too much respect for both of your parents to let anything happen to you."
"I know Earl, but I like to check with them first"
Mee-Mee paused for a second then said "Ok, I'm gamed!"
"Come on me mans over here."
"Oh, you just knew I was going to be ready to go with you?"
"Naw, my man been here waiting for me anyway. I can't stay at things like this long."
"Oh"
Yes, I got her and them. I had he juice laced so she could get sleepy. The plan was in motion. We drove for about 30 minutes talking and joking, then it hit her, and she was out like a light.

"Dummy go to the spot."
"E why you always gotta call me that?"
"Nigga it's just an expression."
"ard, got it."

This nigga really is a dummy. My phone has been blowing up, they must have realized already she was gone damn, they be on that shit. I will answer in a few, but first I got to get securely in place.
We took Mee-Mee in the house and locked her in the room.

246

Lynaia Jordan

"Dummy lets set up."

"Got you E. Do you want to tell Peaches whats going on?"

"For what nigga, she was a part of the problem."

"So, E how you gonna get her back cause this surely aint gonna hurt her."

"Look, I'm gonna say that she made me do all of this. I got this, now finish setting up. Now time to make the video. Put the mask on and point the gun at us both. Say what I wrote on the cards."

Oh, it's on now! We got them.

Lynaia Jordan

Chapter Forty
Meth

Man, my heart was racing so bad, all I could do was keep quite because if Sun knew how I was panicking in the inside

Knock, knock.

"Who is it?"
"It's Meth open the door."
"Ard, nigga hold up."
"Peaches if they are in there, I am going to fuck you up."
"What!"
Peaches opened the door and we pushed pass her.
"Mee-Mee come down here now."
"Hold the fuck up whats going on?"
Sun chimed in "Oh bitch you know whats going on."
Sun started to lunge at Peaches, but I was able to get in between them both.

"Sun it's not the time for this shit."
"I swear Meth if you and this bitch don't get out of my house, it's going to be some fucking trouble."

Just then Clyde come busing through the door.
"Peaches…"
Oh, shit it's about to go down. Smh.

Lynaia Jordan

"Peaches, Peaches Clyde how in the fuck do you know where this bitch lives."

"Baby listen, I can explain."

I just over talked him and said "Look all of you it's not the time or place. I need to know where my little girl is before I start killing motherfuckers."

"Meth wait what do you mean you thought she was here with Earl?"

"Yeah Peaches she left the repast with him, in a black SUV. The same one I saw following us when you moved you shit back home, and you said it was Keith."

"Meth I swear I don't know where they are, I though Earl was still with you all. Keith is on his way over here he can help us find them."

Just then all of our phones went off except for the friend of Clyde's and Peaches.

Sun just screamed and fell to the floor.

The video was of Earl and Mee-Mee tied up, with tape around their mouths, in a room, on a mattress with a nigga that had a gun to their heads, Mee -Mee was sleep and earl was just moving around trying to talk.

The nigga said" If I don't get 1 million in cash, they both are dead, I am going to start with the little nigga then the pretty little bitch. After I fuck her. Don't call the police, if you get them involved, they dead, if you talk to any police they dead, trust me it's real, then he hit Earl in the head with the gun and he went to sleep. Come to Carrollton Park, sit on a bench in front of the bus station, leave the bag there, a homeless man is going to pick it up, if anyone follows him, they are dead. You got 48 hours."

"What the fuck? Peaches where is your phone, see if you got the message too."

"No, I didn't receive anything.'
Clyde jumped and started to chock peaches.
"why the fuck not, it's your son they got. You want to get back us so bad you would stoop this low."

"Clyde let her go!" Sun screamed
" Why baby you know she is behind this."
"I don't know who to believe all I know is yall better get this money together now and get my damn baby back. I just loss my mother, I can't lose her too."

Once Peaches caught her breath she yelled out.

"Clyde you are a bitch ass nigga. If I wanted to get at you or your fucking wife, I didn't need it to be at the safety of my son. Nigga what you forgot!"

Clyde had the dick look on his face.

Lynaia Jordan

"Yeah nigga you lucky this shit is going on cause the cat would be out the bag today bitch!"

"Peaches, Peaches that enough! This is not about you and Clyde or even you and Sun it's about getting our children back. So, let me go over to the Car Wash see how much I got on hand and I'm going to call the bank and see what I can get out of there by Monday afternoon. Clyde, Sun and Peaches you all should do the same."

"Clyde, I got 50 grand that I can give to you."
"Thanks Percy, thanks man. We have to figure out who is behind this."
"Clyde seriously whoever it is has been watching us for a while and they might still be so advice you to just get the money so we can get the kids back."

"Meth you are right."

Clyde tried to pick Sun up and she looked at him and said "You disgust me, I am done with this marriage, get the fucking money together then go get ya shit and get the fuck out of my house and my life. I tried to tell myself that it wasn't true, but I knew it and that's why I don't feel no gilt. Now go get the money! Come on Meth lets go see what you can come up with."

I didn't say another word, I just walked to the car. My gut was telling, me that Sun was fed up and if she is its really over. Thank you Peaches.

Lynaia Jordan

Chapter Forty-One
Sun

I can't believe this shit! One summer back into Baltimore and my life is flipped upside down. My mother is gone, my daughter is kidnapped, my husband is sleeping with my enemy, and my sister hates me. I dare to ask whats next.

We got the money together and Meth is going to make the drop. We asked Peached not to tell Keith about this because we just wanted the kids back safe.

"Meth get them back baby please."

He walked over to me and gave me a kiss and said, I promise to get our little girl back if that's the last thing I do. Sun, I want you to wait at your mother's house its nothing you can do here."

"Meth, I just can't sit around and wait. I just can't." I began to cry.
"Look Sun, this is important, because as soon as they get the money, they can release the kids and the first place they gonna go is here to ya mothers house."

"Ok Meth you are right, please call me as soon as it is done."

Lynaia Jordan

Soon as I said that my phone wrong. It was an unknown number.

"Hello"

"Go to Carroll Park right now, drop the bag off the homeless man will give you a phone, take the phone and wait for my call. Anything goes wrong they are dead."

"Wait please let me talk to her!"

"No, if everything goes right you will see her."

"Ok, it will be Meth dropping off the money."

"Ok. that's fine. Now go."

The call ended.

"Meth, please hurry, please."

"I got it Sun don't worry."

When Meth left, I was a wreck, I walked to the bar and got me a drink, that the only thing I could do.

"Junior and Joy come here please."

"Yeah Ma I'm here. Whats going on."

"I need to tell you both something. First, I would like to start with you Junior. I love you so much my prince. You are half my world. You and your sister mean the world to me and I will do anything to keep you protected. That's why I moved out of Baltimore, so that I can protect you from Jealousy and hate that people had for me. I'm sorry Junior that I failed you."

"Ma. Don't talk like that you didn't fail me or Mesha she was just hard headed and wanted to do what she wanted to so."

Lynaia Jordan

"Joy, my sister, I'm sorry for leaving but that was the only way I knew how to cope with the pain Baltimore gave me. I missed you and mommy like crazy. That's why when this is all over, I am leaving so that you won't have to go through no more pain. I know you want to be close to mommy, you can have everything. I just want you to forgive me for being selfish."

"Sun, I forgive you now you need to get yourself together so when MeeMee comes through that door you will be ready to embrace her."

I began to cry, "Thank you so much Joy, I'm going to take a bath before they get back."

"Yes, relax this may be a long night sis."

She was right, I am drunk and no god to anyone, Meth have been gone for hours, haven't answered his phone or anything. I'm just lost right now. Just then my phone wrong.

"Hello"

"Hello, mommy"

I dropped the phone it was MeeMee. She is whispering

Lynaia Jordan

"Mee-Mee are you ok baby."

"Yes, ma, can you hear me."

"Yes, baby I can hear you."

"Ma its Earl, Ma its Earl, he left the phone please tell daddy be careful, I'm in a room inside of a vacant house, I don't know where it is. I will try to call you again, if the notice the phone missing, he might kill me."

"Baby listen keep the phone on until it goes dead so I can hear everything."

"Ma here he comes, I love you ma, I love you."

Mee-Mee dropped the hone and put it under the covers.

"A Mee-Mee you hungry?"

"No Earl, why are you holding me here."

"I'm not holding you, I'm sorry MeeMee this was the only way."

"Earl, you told me you cared for me."

"I do but it's crazy how money can make you do crazy stuff."

"Earl wait where are we and when are you going to let me go."

"I will let you go in a few as soon as your peoples do the right thing."

"Oh your step father and my mother is in a secret relationship. And your mother and father are in one too. They are really the ones to blame."

Lynaia Jordan

All I could hear Mee Mee do is scream "Liar, liar, you are to blame, and you will pay."

He rushed over to her and said it real quiet, "No, you all will pay."

Then the phone hung up.
I dropped the hone and screamed and cried and screamed,
Meth wasn't answering so I called Clyde

"Clyde, Earl has MeeMee she called me Clyde what should I do."
"Sun, I told you peaches was behind this, I am going to take care of it."
"Take care of it Clyde, I'm tired."
When I said those words, I knew what was about to happen.
Just then Meth walked in the bathroom.

Chapter Forty-Two
Clyde

It's been two days since I have talked to Sun, she has gotten Joy and my mother to communicate for us. The phone rang. When I hung up that phone, I know what has to be done, all of them have to go.

"Percy meet me at Peaches house, gear up nigga it's time to go to war."

When Percy pulled up at Peaches house, he was dressed in all black ready to go.
"My nigga, listen she is going to beg for her life, but we have to get the truth out of her."

"Clyde look, just make sure you can handle whats about to happen because it's not going to be pretty."
Knock, Knock!
"Who is it?"
"It's me Peaches Clyde."
"Clyde what do you want."
"Girl just open the door you done fucked everything else up."
"I don't want to you crazy."
I just kicked the door in, and Peaches went flying to the floor. I smacked her across her face,
"Now tell me where your son is?"
"Clyde, I swear I don't know."

257

Lynaia Jordan

"You are lying."
"Clyde please you are hurting, me, I promise you I don't know."

"Bitch all you do is lie."
"Oh, please Clyde, Please, I swear on our unborn child I don't know. Why would I give up my saving to help yall to get them back?"

"What… Percy wait yo, wait."

Peaches face was bloody, and she was bleeding from the mouth too.
"Peaches what do you mean."

"Clyde, my revenge to Sun was have a baby by you, give you your first born, like she took that away from me with Meth. My plan worked cause I went to the doctors today and they said I was pregnant. I was going to tell you once the kids were back."

She started to spit up blood.
"Clyde, I need to get to a hospital, please, help me and the baby."
I just stood there looking at her.

"Yo Percy, leave yo, please just go. This never happened."
"What my nigga."
"Percy just leave!"

"Peaches come on, let's go."
"Clyde, I can't walk, I think my leg is broken."

258

Lynaia Jordan

"Aw Peaches, I'm sorry, I'm going to protect you, I'm sorry, I pray our baby is ok."

"I know, I'm tired of this shit Clyde, I want this to be right this time go around."

"Don't worry Peaches it will be."

I carried Peaches into the hospital and told them she was assaulted by a group of females. She went along with the story. I'm going to have to figure out a way to tell Sun, I have to make shit right for my unborn child. I have to.

Lynaia Jordan

Chapter Forty-Three
Meth

Just like he said a homeless man was waiting for me to give him the bag. He handed me a cellphone and told me to wait for the phone call. The whole ride back to Sun's mothers house I was trying to think who could have been behind all of this shit. I have no clue.

"Sun, Sun are you ok?"
She was sitting in the middle of the bathroom floor crying naked.
"Sun baby get up."
"Meth, I did something bad."
"Sun what did you do?"
"I told Clyde to take out Peaches because Mee-Mee called me, and I heard Earl saying we all are going to pay."
"What, I'm gonna kill her myself. Call Clyde right now. We have to wait for this phone to ring."

"Clyde where are you."
"Sun I am at the hospital with Peaches she was jumped, also Sun she doesn't have anything to do with this."
I had to jump in the conversation cause this nigga is pissing me off.
"How the fuck do you know that?"
"Who's this Meth?"
"Yeah who else would it be."

Lynaia Jordan

"Look nigga, I just know, now we got to find out where Earl is with Mee-Mee and fast. What happened when you dropped off the bread?"

"They gave me a cell phone."

"Look Meth, I'm gonna call Keith and have him tract the number, I will call you right back and tell you what to do."

"Clyde is Peaches ok."

"Hopefully she gonna be fine, her and the baby."

He hung up and all I could do was look at Sun's face. Dejavu all over again.

"Sun, I'm sorry."

"It's ok Meth, at least I know the truth, the only person I'm worried about is our daughter. Please Meth get her back safe."

Just then the phone rang.

"Hello"

"Yeah, everything is good, now take the phone and go to the GPS and it will lead you to them. Thanks for doing business with you."

"Them, Earl you mean my daughter, I know it's you Earl, but your mother is in the hospital on her death bed thanks to you. You won't be able to spend it."

Lynaia Jordan

I hung the phone up and me and Sun rant o the car and turned on the GPS of the phone. I took us to Bel Air, Maryland a house for sale.

"Sun hand me the guns out that compartment."
        "Meth give me one, I'm coming with you."
"Ok but I need for you to cover me outside."

My cellphone started to ring.

"Hello"
"Hey Meth, this is Keith, Clyde called and told me everything, call me from that other phone and tell me where you are.

"I'm on my way inside the house to get my baby girl. The address is 2807 Main Street, Bel Air, Maryland. I can't wait for you Keith."

"Ok, I'm on the way, I am like five minutes away."

When I hung up the phone, I got a funny feeling in my stomach, I turned and told Sun "I love you and no matter what happens after this moment, me and you will be forever King and Queen. Take care of our kids including Malik please Sun I beg you."

        "Meth we are going to raise all of our kids in our house in Georgia and keep our family strong and together."

262

Lynaia Jordan

I gave Sun the gun and told her to keep an eye out for anything suspicious, "Oh Sun Keith is coming."

"ok, baby hurry up."

I walked slowly into the house; all the lights were out so I called out. "Mee-Mee, baby where are you."

"Daddy, I'm in the room upstairs."

I ran up the steps as fast as I can and when I opened the door, I saw my baby, tied up to the bed. Just then I was hit across my head with a gun.

Lynaia Jordan

Chapter Forty-Four
Sun

Things will never be the same. I had to come to the funeral and watch them put the body in the ground. It was the fact of seeing gave me security. I know that they are hurting, but what about all the hurt, everyone caused me. I am not a selfish, heartless, person but Baltimore has turned me cold.

You see Meth gave me the gun and when he did all I could think of was murder, so I called the police, I didn't want to handle this situation anymore. Then I saw Keith pull up on the side of the house, but he was alone. Why he didn't call for back up that didn't sit right with me so, I got out the car. I followed him in the house, I could hear Meth call out for Mee-Mee, her screaming, then quiet. I creeped up the steps and saw Earl and Keith tying Meth up.

"What the fuck are yall doing?"
Keith said, "Earl hit the lights grab her."
"I swear Earl if you cut off them lights, I'm gonna kill you."
"Earl, she doesn't know how to use a gun cut them off."
"Keith shut the fuck up., Why are you doing this. What did I do to yall?"

Lynaia Jordan

"Sun you couldn't just let Peaches have her way, because of you this boy had to be taken care of by a junkie father, never getting to know his mother, I loved you Sun and you just left me for him."

"Keith and Earl, I am sorry, this can be over just let them go and we will not say anything we will leave Baltimore for good. Yall can keep the money."

They both started to laugh.

"Oh Ms. Sun we are going to keep the money and kill all of you. No one knows you are here."

"Earl that's what you think."
Just then Earl jumped and cut the lights out and gunfire just went off in the room. I fell to the floor and fired towards Earl. The next thing I knew, I was in a hospital room with police guarding my door. I panicked and started to push the button.
Screaming "Nurse, Nurse where is my daughter, where is Meth."

"Calm down Mrs. Jordan, please calm down, I will have the officer to come and talk to you."

"Hello, Mrs. Jordan, I am office Delbridge, I would like to ask you a few questions about what happened last week."

"Sir, is my daughter and children father ok."

Lynaia Jordan

"Ok, what is the name of your children father?"
　　"Methon Washington."
I started to cry, I knew they killed him, I knew it.
"Oh ok, so yes, Mr. Washington and Ms. Washington are ok. They are waiting out in the hallway waiting to see you. I just needed to be the first person to talk to you so I can get a clear picture of what happened."
Thank you, God,

"Ok officer, I can tell you everything."
　　After I told him what happened, he told me that Keith was killed in gunfire with the police, and the young man died from his car crashing into a tree.

"Please, let me see my family."
"Very well, that this all I needed from you."

Meth, Junior, Mee-Mee and Joy came in the room. They were so happy that to see me. I was shot in my side and leg, but they were only flesh wounds nothing hit anything major.

Meth said, "Sun baby, I'm so glad you are ok, they wouldn't tell us anything."

"Mommy, yes, thank you ma for coming for me."
"Ma, I was so worried about you, but I always knew you were a soldier."
"Sis you had all of us worried, you wouldn't wake up."

"I'm glad to see all of you, where is Clyde?"

"Sun he is at the hospital with Peaches, she was beat really bad and had to have surgery on her jaw. He been there, he said that she is pregnant with his child."

"Oh well, things happen for a reason. I am not questioning nothing, and nothing surprises me. I just want to get out of this hospital and live."

"Sun, I promise you I will protect our family forever!"

"Meth did they identify the body in the truck as Earl's."

"Sun, I honestly don't know, it was another person, but we don't know who it was. Since he never went to the doctors or even had a record, the couldn't identify the body in the car so we just assumed it was Earl."

"Meth, we must find out. When is Keith funeral, I want to attend and also the memorial for Earl?"

"It's tomorrow, Peaches had insurance on Keith and Earl Jr."

Lynaia Jordan

Chapter Forty-Five
Earl

I gotta get out of here, I'm just gonna go for it. I jumped to cut out the lights and ran out the house to the truck, my nigga was already sitting there waiting.

"Yo pull off this hit is hot!"

"What the fuck E, you said this was going to be easy."

"We got the money and we on our way now just drive."

We pulled off and the police was pulling up.

"Nigga stop looking in the rear view and pay attention."

"E let me drive."

"Watch out for that can."

This nigga swerved into a tree. I just jumped out the truck and ran to a neighbor's yard. The truck went up in flames. I could hear him calling for me to help but I couldn't it was too late.

"Damn, Damn, Damn, what did I do, he didn't deserve this."

I turned and kept on walking, I got the money and the revenge. I think Sun is dead, I know I shot her. I gonna make

Lynaia Jordan

me a new life, fuck all of them and if I decide to reappear, they better continue to watch their back!

…………………….....THE END.………………

Lynaia Jordan

Part III

I couldn't imagine a better way than to spend the twins 21st birthday in Cancun, Mexico. Meth and I decided to tell the kids the good news. I haven't heard from Clyde, I guess everything was true about him and Peaches. I was served divorce papers three weeks after the funeral. I was glad that he decided to stay away, because if I ever see him, I'm not sure what I might do. I heard that they had a daughter and they named her Clai'sha. That ghetto ass name. I don't think me, and Meth need any more kids. We have the twins, Malik, which are grown so we can live our life.

"Meth, I'm going to go get some more towels"
      "Ok, baby, bring me back a drink."
"What would you like?"
      "I don't care surprise me."
Walking back from the getting the towels and drinks I felt someone watching me walk. I turned and looked and didn't see anyone I knew.
      "Meth, come on let's go to the indoor pool, it's a lot of creepy men looking at me."

      "Oh, let them stare baby, you are beautiful and mines."
"Excuse me Mr. Washington, the gentlemen that's sitting over there sent you these drinks over."
      "See baby, you got them sending us free drinks. Waiter, what gentleman?"

270

Lynaia Jordan

"I'm sorry Mr. Washington he is gone."
"Meth that's creepy."
"Could you describe him.to me please, I would like to thank him."
"He is tall, dark skin with a burn on the side of his face."
We both looked at each other and said, "Oh Hell No!!"

Lynaia Jordan